Cosmic Crime Stories
March 2024

Edited by Tyree Campbell

Cosmic Crime Stories
March 2024
Edited by Tyree Campbell

All rights reserved. No part of this book may be reproduced or transmitted in any form or by any means, electronic or mechanical, including photocopying or recording or by any information storage and retrieval systems, without expressed written consent of the authors and/or artists.

Cosmic Crime Stories is a work of fiction. Names, characters, places, and incidents are products of the authors' imaginations. Any resemblance to actual events or persons, living or dead, is entirely coincidental.

Story and illustration copyrights owned by the respective authors.

Cover art "The 7:15 Adventure" by Laura Givens
Cover design by Laura Givens

First Printing March 2024
Hiraeth Publishing
http://hiraethsffh.com/
@HiraethPublish1

Visit http://hiraethsffh.com/ for online science fiction, fantasy, horror, scifaiku, and more. Also visit the Hiraeth Publishing bookstore for paperbacks, magazines, anthologies, and chapbooks. Support the small, independent press...

Contents

Short Stories

7   Outpost 9000 by Keyla Damaer

23   The Lizard's Kiss by David Castlewitz

41   Hidden Talents by Lisa Timpf

72   Customer Satisfaction by Rosie Oliver

96   A Way Out by Sarina Bosc

100   Sisters by Toni Artuso

120   Angling by Jacob Hazzard

Articles

68   The Astronaut Always Rings Twice – reviewed by Lisa Timpf

127   Who's Who?

Iuliae: Past Tense
By Tyree Campbell

Two sisters of the Iulius Family have run away from the restrictions and rules of their settlement on a remote world, and embark on a journey of discovery, to learn what to do with their new-found freedom. Along the way, they become smugglers, and opponents of human trafficking, and become fugitives from the law and from the corporations.

Iulia Sexta, the younger of the two sisters, is suffering from an identity crisis. Is it gender dysphoria? Was she supposed to be a man? Is that why she likes girls? Or is a ghost from one of her previous lives now trying to haunt his way back into the living by taking over her body and mind?

With both the past and the present pursuing them, Iulia Tertia and Iulia Sexta find their future under constant attack. Doing the right thing is not only difficult at best, but may well result in their deaths. What to do? One thing at a time…

https://www.hiraethsffh.com/product-page/iuliae-past-tense-by-tyree-campbell

A Little Help, Please

In the world of the small indie press we fight a never-ending battle for attention to our work, as writers and in publishing. Here's an example: big publishers [you know who they are] have gobs of $$$ that they can devote to advertising and marketing. Here at Hiraeth Publishing, our advertising budget consists of the deposits for whatever soda bottles and aluminum cans we can find alongside the highways. Anti-littering laws make our task even more difficult . . . ☺

That's where YOU come in. YOU are our best promoter. YOU are the one who can tell others about us. Just send 'em to our website, tell them about our store. That's all. Just that.

Of course, we don't mind if you talk us up. We're pretty good, you know. We have some award-winning and award-nominated writers and artists, plus other voices well-deserving to be heard [not everyone wins awards, right?] but our publications are read-worthy nevertheless.

That number once again is:
www.hiraethsffh.com

Friend us on Facebook at Hiraeth Publishing
Follow us on Twitter at @HiraethPublish1

Outpost 9000
Keyla Damaer

Estrella straightened the blue jacket of the security division's uniform as she strode to the lift, her long black hair pulled into a twisted top knot. As the lift moved from ground level to the operations floor, she took a moment to admire the outstanding engineering work the International Space Agency—ISA—had accomplished in expanding the sixteen modules of the International Space Station into this impressive structure.

The new layout resembled an arachnid, with a central body rising on five different levels and six mega legs extending from it.

The lift came to a sudden stop with a thud, and the doors opened, allowing Estrella to step out.

Commander Altamura stood near the tactical station, engaged in a conversation with the tactical officer as he stroked his goatee, never a good sign.

Estrella approached the couple and saluted. "Lieutenant Kutyna reporting for duty."

Altamura inspected her uniform and raised his eyes to meet hers. Her stature often intimidated men, but not this one. "Follow me."

They strode to his spacious office on the other side of the room and disappeared inside.

"As you were, Lieutenant." He settled into his leather chair and gestured for her to do the same.

She sat, her hands folded in her lap.

"We seem to have a situation on Outpost 9000."

Bad news indeed.

She leant forwards, keen to discover what the situation was, and what she could do about it.

"Two days ago, the communication array stopped sending signals."

That was odd. Normally, an outpost would be sending though all kind of data about the mission, the ship, and the crew's vital signs, not to mention the crew's private messages. They needed regular reports, not these kind of interruptions.

"Without any communications, we don't even know if they're still alive," Altamura explained.

Estrella nodded. She was the team's most qualified expert. It made sense that they would send her if there was an issue with the communication array. "So you want me to go and check it out?"

"And fix it. If you can't fix the array go to the Outpost. I want to know that they are unharmed. We can't have them losing touch with their loved ones or feeling cut off".

She wanted to object. Going alone wasn't a good idea if things had gone awry at Outpost 9000. She was only a technician. But soldiers didn't argue orders. She straightened up in the chair and locked eyes with him. Soldiers didn't argue orders. "I'm ready to go, sir."

Altamura nodded. "Repair the array and investigate what happened to our crew. You leave in thirty minutes with the Sputnik Module. Dismissed."

***

You put a spell on me, 'n now I'm yours...

The famous song from two centuries ago played on the computer, as it did every day at 0700, waking Martin.

His schedule remained the same every day on Outpost 9000. It had been that way since he had arrived there, one hundred and fifty-seven days before.

A yawn stretched his mouth wide open. He unstrapped himself from the safety of his bed. He adjusted his Clark Gable mustache in front of the mirror while still humming along with the recorded music. The lower artificial gravity made everything feel like watching a video in slow motion.

Once refreshed, he dressed and combed his midnight black hair. He had a gander at the red stains on his gray coveralls and shrugged. It didn't matter. Nobody bothered about uniforms here.

The station was unusually quiet when he slipped out of his cabin. *Perhaps they slept in,* he thought. He chuckled.

When he passed by the operations, he greeted Patrick O'Hara, the chief engineer, who sat at his console. He didn't reply, but Martin shrugged it off. O'Hara usually talked too much, anyway.

Martin drifted toward the mess hall, where he consumed a low-fat, energy breakfast in solitude. Only then did he proceed to his lab, where he spent the entire day working on bacteria samples.

The ISA had completed the outpost's construction two years earlier in a region of space with a planetoid inhabited by alien bacteria. Martin, like hundreds of other biologists, had enlisted to take part in the program. Who wouldn't want to space travel?

Of course, this honor came at a cost. It meant being isolated from the world for six months, in addition to the time needed to travel back to the ISS, and the subsequent debriefing at Pushkin on Earth.

At precisely 1700, he secured the vial in his hands and left the lab, muttering his favorite song.

You put a spell on me, 'n now I'm yours...

Anya Gagarin, the brunette commander of the settlement, sat at the head of the rectangular table in the mess hall, the same table they used for briefings.

"It's good to see you, Dr. Logan. I was waiting for you." She sat on her chair as if impaled on it.

"Oh, sorry for being late, Commander. You could have started without me." Martin took the time to admire the way her eyes sparkled like *grandidierite* for a few more seconds.

"I detest eating alone, you know that." She leaned toward him, looking up from under her long lashes with a coy smile.

Oddly enough, Martin wasn't the only one who was late. O'Hara and Commander Lieutenant Chrétien, the security officer, were also absent. Martin pulled out two synthesized meals from the cabinet.

"I bet you will miss me once I am back on Earth." He served her meal and sat down to the woman's left.

"I most definitely will, Doctor. Have you decided what to get your nephew?" Gagarin drummed her fingers on the table.

His mouth curled up, as his mind went back to the time spent with his nephew, Jesse, who awaited his return. Martin and his wife had taken in the boy after his parents died in a train accident when Jesse was only seven. Martin loved his nephew as if he were his own son, and he couldn't wait to be reunited with him once his replacement arrived from the ISS in the Sputnik Module. Martin would return to the station in the second module—the MIR—and then back to Earth.

"No, I have not. I'm worried I won't have time to shop if I'm stationed in Pushkin while I readapt to Earth's gravity."

Gagarin hadn't touched her meal. Martin observed her hands, splayed on the table like they were glued to it. Maybe she wasn't hungry, he decided before turning his mind back to the problem of returning home empty-handed.

"Catherine Palace's the biggest mall in the area," Gagarin suggested. "I'm sure you'll find the right gift for him there. Or maybe—" She paused. "You could get him some samples of the pretty rocks from the Anabara Caves. You told me he collects rocks, right? I know someone in Saint Petersburg who has authentic ones at fair prices. It's easy to get there as it's right by Pushkin."

"Rocks, yes. Jesse collects them." His mind wandered to his collection of rocks, neatly catalogued and displayed on shelves throughout his house on Earth.

She snorted. "Have you sent this week's report to the base yet?" She changed the topic without warning.

Why does she always have to talk about work?

"No. We are still having issues with the communications array. I cannot send too much data with the long-range communication equipment. O'Hara forbade me from doing so," Martin explained the issue for the third time.

"Then he'll have to check what's wrong with the array manually."

The journey from the outpost to the array took ten terrestrial hours. The round trip, along with the time needed to repair the array, would keep their chief engineer away for about twenty-four hours in the best-case scenario. No way they could manage without their engineer for that long in this godforsaken place for a second. Martin was glad Patrick backed him up on this matter.

However, Gagarin considered the array a priority.

"It is your call. I am just a biologist." Annoyed by her persistence, Martin stood, cleaned the table, and left Gagarin in the mess hall, stopping by Patrick, who was still sitting at his console.

"She is at it again. Good luck!" he said.

"Thanks, man. See you tomorrow."

Martin retired to his private quarters, muttering the words of his favorite song, "*You put a spell on me, 'n now I'm yours—*"

***

Ten hours and thirty minutes after leaving the ISS, the Sputnik Module docked at the communication array.

Estrella donned the environmental suit, a lighter version of the ones used during her training four years before. Only the helmet remained as uncomfortable as ever, forcing her to undo her bun and stash her hairpin in her back pocket.

When she picked up the emergency repair kit to secure it to her suit, she asked herself whether she had donned the gloves at all as the feel of the handle was so natural.

Like touching things with my bare hands.

Estrella flew to the decompression room, sealed the lock, and activated the process.

Once it was complete, she turned on the gravity boots. They snapped onto the surface with a clang, but only a slight vibration passed through the heavy helmet.

Finally, she opened the outer lock and stepped onto the array. The endless view was breathtaking and could cause dizziness. To be on the safe side, Estrella focused on her only visible reference: the array itself.

The main power regulator was twenty-three meters ahead. It was only a few minutes of EVA, but the environmental suit and lack of gravity made it an experience even for the most trained soldier.

Step by step, without gazing into the endless darkness of space, she reached the voltage regulator. As expected, it was offline. With the tools wired to her suit, Estrella attempted to bring it back online, but nothing she did worked: the array remained offline. One last option remained: to remove the panel and check the circuits behind it. Perhaps there had been an overload, although the logs hadn't recorded one. Screw after screw, she slowly detached the panel and secured everything to her suit. She expected to find burned wires, but her mouth formed a silent circle of surprise when she found them cut through.

Despite the even temperature inside her suit, a drop of sweat ran down her neck.

Someone spent a lot of time removing the panel and replacing it, after cutting the wires.

But who? And why? There was no one out here, no human in any direction for ten hours. Sweat beaded across her forehead. First contact with a hostile species alone and in the middle of nowhere didn't fall into Estrella's bucket list. But there had been no signs of intelligent life forms thus far, and she couldn't exclude sabotage. The thought was equally unsettling.

The round trip required twenty hours, and no one could leave the outpost without their prolonged absence being noticed. If the saboteur came from Outpost 9000, it meant they had incapacitated or even killed the crew.

She set that dreadful thought aside. What she needed was a new voltage regulator block and a team to assist her in replacing it, but even with the right equipment, it wasn't a one-person job. For the first time, she wished she had argued with Altamura's order to send her alone.

Estrella glanced down at the emergency repair kit in dismay. Without the array, she wouldn't know whether the crew were safe.

She returned to the module, removed the suit, and sent a subspace message to the ISS with a brief report.

***

"Outpost 9000, come in. This is Lieutenant Kutyna. I'm initiating maneuvers for docking at the available docking port," Estrella said into the comms.

No one answered. What if everyone was dead? A niggling fear swelled inside her, despite her training. Again, she reckoned Altamura had made a terrible mistake sending her alone.

Then her training kicked in. She straightened her shoulders and repeated the message.

"Commander Kutyna, I read you clear. Initiate docking procedure. You are welcome on board," a male voice said, coming from the comm.

"Who's speaking?" It wasn't O'Hara. His Irish accent was unmistakable, not to mention his predilection toward waffling.

"This is Doctor Logan. Chief O'Hara is unavailable at the moment."

At least they weren't all dead. There was someone to talk to and get an explanation from. What was so important to keep the engineer away from his post at such a delicate moment, though?

"I expect a report from each one of you ASAP. Kutyna out."

Her mind mused for a few more seconds on O'Hara's reasons, but she couldn't dwell while maneuvering to the dock. It was one of the hardest parts of space travel.

Before leaving the module, she took her bag and checked the contents: a medical scanner, a torch, and a sonic gun. The artificial lights of the Sputnik gave the weapon a sinister look.

She clipped it behind her back, underneath the blue jacket, and scanned the outpost for life signs. The tool detected two others. *It's okay. The scanner wouldn't detect someone inside the MIR docked on the other side of the outpost or someone performing a spacewalk in that same area,* she told herself, even though the uneasiness of solitude washed over her.

Hopefully, there was a logical explanation for the strange events of the last couple of days.

When she left the module, no one was waiting for her.

Where's Commander Anya Gagarin? It was standard procedure to greet a new member of the crew, whatever the reason for their arrival. Besides, a new face breaking the solitary routine should be a welcome change—the four crew members had lived in isolation for months.

Then she spotted a man drifting toward her and recognized Dr. Logan from the picture on his file. His appearance reassured her. Soon, she would have some answers.

"Welcome aboard, Lieutenant Kutyna. We were not expecting you," he said.

They pushed themselves toward operations, along the corridor in the sleeping area.

"I know. Where are the others?"

Logan shrugged. "Chief O'Hara is at his console, as usual. Commander Gagarin is in the mess hall and Lieutenant Commander Chrétien is inside the MIR. She was checking some ... things with Patrick. I never understand them when they talk technological gibberish," Logan said with a nervous smile.

If O'Hara was at his post, why hadn't he replied to her message before? And why hadn't her scanner detected his life sign? Something didn't add up, but she couldn't put a finger on it.

"I am glad you arrived. I am more than ready to get back to Earth. Some business is waiting for me." Logan slowed down, moving behind her.

What was Logan talking about? His mission wasn't over yet. She spun around, but the scientist was gone.

A groan came from the mess hall, just two steps ahead on her left.

Estrella's hand bolted to her weapon. She wielded it and pushed herself inside, gasping at the sight.

Commander Gagarin sat tethered to a chair, her hands stuck to the table, held in place by two knives cutting through her palms. A tray of untouched rotten food lay anchored on the table in front of her, along with a gray blob of something that appeared to be food.

She muttered something, but Estrella couldn't understand a word. Only then did she recognize the blob of food and wrestled with the urge to vomit. It was Gagarin's tongue.

She floated to the commander. "Stay calm. I'm here to help." She scanned the woman, finding traces of several drugs in her bloodstream: high dosages of coagulants, sleeping drugs, and antibiotics. A thorough scan of Gagarin's tongue suggested someone had cut it out about three days before, a gelatinous substance above it kept the festering at bay.

Was Logan responsible for this?

Estrella set aside her instinct to help the commander. First thing first, she must assess the situation. Gagarin's life wasn't in immediate danger from her wounds. Estrella held the commander's chin with her hand and lifted it gently. "Gagarin, I'll be right back. I'm not leaving you behind. Understood?"

The woman's stupefied eyes were half-closed. She replied to her question with more moans.

With the gun in one hand and the scanner in the other, Estrella checked again for human life signs. Now there was only one other than hers. Where did Logan go? And where were the others? From the mess hall, she launched herself to the opposite corridor, toward the other docking site where the MIR module should be. The endless fight against microgravity slowed her down.

The module was where it was supposed to be, but it wasn't empty. Lieutenant Chrétien lay inside with a slit throat.

"What the *frieck*?" she exclaimed, pulling herself toward the mess hall, this time taking the third corridor leading to the labs and operations. Nothing looked out of the ordinary in Logan's lab.

Everything was as tidy and clean as she would expect in a scientific environment.

Perhaps his logs would tell her more.

She fidgeted with the console to override the security codes with her own. The last log recorded just before her arrival claimed he had just sent a message to Jesse about his return. More logs mentioned his reunion with his nephew. It sounded like an obsession. But most of all, it made no sense. Logan's nephew was dead.

It dawned on her that Logan had lost his marbles. Either he was responsible for Chrétien's death and Gagarin's wounds or he was helping the person—human or alien—responsible for them.

She searched for an explanation, skimming older logs, but Logan kept repeating over and over that he was returning home soon, and in most audio logs, he kept singing a song: *You put a spell on me, 'n now I'm yours....*

At last, she found a three-day-old log where Logan explained how he felt like a new person after breaking a vial with one bacterium he was studying. In the same log, he told the story of his trip to the array. To fix it, according to him.

Estrella squeezed her watery eyes shut and clamped her left hand over her mouth to suppress a groan of fear, frustration, and determination to not end up like her colleague Chrétien. Contamination was the most plausible explanation to Logan's behaviour. What if he were contagious? She could be infected as well, by now. And what would happen if Logan went back to the ISS? He could contaminate everyone.

"Frieck!"

The sound of music filled the air, interrupting her mental debate. It came from outside the lab.

You put a spell on me, 'n now I'm yours...

Still holding the gun, she drifted to operations.

Chief Patrick O'Hara was indeed sitting at his console, with his back at the entrance, but he had a hole in the upper side of his skull. A multiphase screwdriver with stains of blood hung in the air just above the corpse. Splinters of bones and pieces of brain danced around it.

Estrella's stomach churned, and despite her attempt to take a grip, she threw up. The spasms didn't stop even after her stomach had emptied.

She rested her hand against a bulkhead to keep steady and took deep breaths to regain control of herself.

The music playing from the internal comms brought her back to reality and her duty.

She scanned O'Hara to assess the time of death, trying to ignore the gore and the smell of her fresh puke to the best of her abilities. The results were consistent with Logan's trip to the array. She ignored the corpse and opened a channel to the Sputnik, suspecting Logan was there.

"Logan, come in!"

"Oh, Lieutenant Kutyna! It is a pleasure to hear from you," the scientist responded with a cheery voice.

"Logan, where are you going? To Jesse?"

"Yes, I am. Did Gagarin tell you so? I told her to shush, but she would not listen to me. Women do not understand when it is time to shut the frieck up." He spat, with a sudden change in his mood.

"Did you kill O'Hara and Chrétien?" Kutyna asked.

He laughed. "Kill? Why would I kill them? They are not dead. I was talking to them just before you arrived." Martin's voice was quiet now.

"Logan, can you hear me?" The module was still docked. If she locked the clamps, all she needed to do was to incapacitate Logan and assist Gagarin while waiting for someone to get there.

Laughing at the joke, she pushed O'Hara off the seat and took his place, but nothing she tried unlocked the console.

Frieck!

"Logan, come in!" she ordered.

No answer. The only sound was the music playing in the background.

She turned around, sensing a presence behind her. Something hard hit her chin, and everything went black.

***

"I do not know why they sent a security officer instead of the scientist who is supposed to relieve me. Whatever the reason, I am leaving. Jesse has been waiting for me for too long. I will give him a gift from Pushkin, so he will forgive me." Logan's high-pitched voice shouted inside her ear, waking Estrella.

Her head pounded, and her chin hurt, but those weren't her major problems. A long, tight rope kept her bound to a mess hall chair with her hands behind her. Next to her sat Gagarin, her head leaning on her chest. Was she dead, too?

Logan was out of control. Sweat leaped to her skin as her heart drummed in her chest.

She snapped herself out of her panic, thankful for her training, and eyed the scientist across from the table.

"Logan, your Jesse is dead. He died two years ago. You went on leave to recover for six months. Only then the doctors declared you fit for duty," she said, trying to make him see reason.

"You, Chrétien, and Gagarin are in league together, but I know what I know, and you will not stop me." Logan spoke with confidence.

He twirled his head and pointed his finger at Gagarin. "Stop bothering me with your chit-chat, Gagarin, or I will cut your tongue. I do not want to listen to your nonsense any longer," he snarled at the pinioned woman, who was either unconscious or dead.

"Logan, Gagarin's tongue is on the table. She can't talk. If you are hearing voices, they must be inside your head."

Logan pushed himself towards her and thrust his clenched fists close to her face. "Are you talking inside my head?"

Estrella stiffened, restraining herself from flinching to keep her fear at bay. "No, I'm not, but the others are. We're alone here."

The thought sent a shiver down her spine. She was alone with a murderer infected by alien bacteria.

She bit her lower lip to fight back a panic attack.

Logan's head shook with so much vigor she feared it might fly off at some point. "We are not alone. Gagarin is here, and Patrick is at his post." Logan spat his words.

"What about Chrétien? Where is she?" Estrella asked.

"I do not know. I have not seen her since I returned from the array."

At least, he remembered going to the array. But that didn't change her position. She must buy herself some time and prevent him from leaving the outpost. "Did you sabotage it?"

"I did not. I fixed it." Logan explained, lowering his voice, and sounding as calm as if nothing had happened.

"Logan, you know nothing of engineering. You admitted that yourself when I arrived. How could you fix it?" *Tell me there's still some sense deep down inside you, Logan.*

"I fixed it with Patrick two days ago."

"The MIR can host only one person at a time. Did you kill him?"

"No, Patrick is sitting at his console, working on telemetry as usual. A very boring job, if I must say."

You're hopeless, and I'm doomed.

She eyed Gagarin, but the woman was still unconscious. No help would come from her. Estrella needed to stop the scientist. If Logan was infected with something, she didn't want to be remembered as the person responsible for decimating Earth's population. *If anyone survives.* The thought gave her goosebumps.

"Logan, release me."

"Are you insane? I am not restraining you. You need a doctor, Lieutenant. I will inform the ISS's staff of your condition. Now I really have to go."

No, no, no! You can't leave me here. "Logan, you can't go. You may be contaminated..." *Or have just gone bonkers.*

But Logan wasn't listening. He left the mess hall and headed left.

Noises resembling those of fingers tapping on a console came from operations. The computer emitted bleeps here and there.

Estrella kept her eyes and ears open to what he was doing while fumbling inside a back pocket, looking for a hairpin. And there it was, her precious tool to freedom. With a tight grip on it, she extracted it from the pocket and fidgeted with it to unlock her cuffs.

With her eyes on the door and her ears focused on listening to Logan's noises, she tried to free herself.

The sudden appearance of the assassin startled her. The hairpin slipped through her fingers, and she almost lost her grip on it. But he didn't stop by and drifted toward the sleeping area and the Sputnik. Breathing with relief, she resumed her work.

It took ages to free herself, and when she finally succeeded, Gagarin moaned. Estrella wanted to help her, but first, she must stop the assassin.

With caution, she approached the entrance to the mess hall and peeked in both directions—no sign of Logan—then pushed herself to operations. O'Hara's corpse still floated in the area with his other bloody bits.

Her attention focused on a flashing light on a little screen to the left. It was a countdown. 14:22, 14:21...

The music filled the air from the internal comms.

You put a spell on me, 'n now I'm yours...

"I am sorry, Kutyna, but I could not let you stop me. Gagarin and O'Hara will be in good company. Space can be a lonely place."

Logan. He must be back to the Sputnik.

She cursed again, then set a timer to her wristband to keep track of the time and pushed herself to the mess hall.

"I locked your computer, as you can see. You cannot send messages, Kutyna, and that timer you see...

well, Patrick set that to destroy the outpost. He must have lost it," Logan said from the internal comms.

With the computer locked, she couldn't use it to deactivate the clamping docks and use the MIR to escape. But even if that weren't the case, she wasn't alone, and she had a duty to save Gagarin too.

"I know what you are trying to do, Kutyna. Resign yourself. You cannot leave the outpost, my dear. Someone needs to stay and watch. I am sorry I have to go, but Jesse is waiting for me." Logan said through the speakers. The signal was getting weaker as the Sputnik gained distance.

Estrella hurried to the cabinet beside the main console, grabbing two environmental suits. One for her and one for Gagarin. Then she took the emergency kit: the *cauterspray* was still sealed.

"*You put a spell on me, 'n now I'm yours...*" Logan's voice, singing that odd song above the original music, trailed off.

Gagarin sat with her hands pinned at the table. They gazed at each other—the commander still looking off in a spell. At least, she was awake again.

Estrella removed the blades to free the other woman and cauterized her wounds with the *cauterspray*. Then, while helping her into the environmental suit, she explained the situation and her plan, hoping Gagarin understood her.

After they had donned their suits, she dragged Gagarin all the way to the decompression chamber and manually activated the process. While waiting, she tethered her suit to Gagarin's.

The timer showed 3:57 minutes and counting.

"I must open the hatch manually one minute before the process is over or we won't be able to escape the explosion."

Gagarin put a hand on her arm as if to stop her.
3:39.

The commander didn't look as lucid as she had hoped for. She outranked Estrella, but given her medical condition, Gagarin was in no state to give orders.

"I know it's not recommended, but we can get out one minute before. That will give us time to escape the blast. These suits have little power, but we have to take our chances."

Gagarin shook her head, squeezing Estrella's arm. A grimace of pain accompanied the gesture.

2:12.

"You can file a report about my insubordination if we survive, ma'am." Estrella removed the commander's hand from her arm and checked their suit's propulsion system and the oxygen level, then hoped for the best. "Activate your propulsion when I open the hatch," she said to Gagarin.

When the timer got to 1:07, she opened the hatch. They flew together into outer space, sucked out like two feathers by a vacuum cleaner.

Estrella activated the little propulsive system of her suit through the commands on her suit's wristband.

Feeling lightheaded, she checked the time.

0:39.

She fumbled with the commands on the suit wristband a second time to record a message.

"This is Commander Kutyna from Outpost 9000. Doctor Logan killed both O'Hara and Chrétien. He also sabotaged the communications array and activated a bomb on the outpost going off soon, then escaped with the MIR. Logan seems to be contaminated with some bacteria. He's armed and dangerous. Commander Gagarin and I escaped with two environment suits, but the blast may take us with it in five seconds. Kutyna out."

0:03

She pushed the button to send the subspace message, hoping it would get to the ISS before Logan did.

0:02.

0:01.

0:00.

The Lizard's Kiss
David Castlewitz

Larry Klein stood with his hands in his side pockets. His reptilian partner lumbered over, her huge feet making the floorboards moan, and asked, "Why the sand?"

Turning to her, Klein realized for the Nth time that he wouldn't have known her gender if he hadn't been told. He wouldn't even recognize her in a crowd if she didn't wear a nametag. Materek looked like every other lizard. He couldn't tell one from the other.

"They put the—" He almost used the derogatory term "lizard" but caught himself – "baby in the sandbox." He didn't know more about the cultists who snatched reptilian infants from their homes. It was a widespread phenomenon ripe with rumors.

"This is the first such table I've seen." Materek paused between words, obviously finding it difficult to translate thoughts into English.

Klein surveyed the room. There'd be no clues left behind. No ID dropped on the floor. No forgotten cups foaming with DNA.

"And the babes?" Materek asked, her oval eyes swelling. She blinked, her scaly eyelids closing, then opening, leaving behind a thin transparent film that dissipated after a few seconds. The lizard's way of crying, Klein thought, amused by his partner's display of emotion.

"They don't kill them. Not when they're babies. That comes later."

"Your kind are truly barbarians."

Klein shrugged, wondering what lizard word his partner had translated to "barbarian." The coming of the Reptilians had initially been heralded as Earth's salvation. They cleaned the atmosphere, put a stop to poisoning the environment, established new industries, put down the little wars raging across the planet, and established a new world order.

They came as benefactors when Klein was a boy.

"My suggestion," Materek said, "is to visit a parental pod that reported a stolen baby."

"We got the police report. We know the particulars."

"I am new to this, Larry Klein. My ideas may not have merit to you. Still, these are my kind that are being stolen and killed. Allow me to investigate my way. Let's go to the point of origin of the crime and seek evidence there."

Klein sighed. Investigating these things was mere formality, but he got stuck with a partner who took it seriously. Worse, her stilted diction irritated him.

Outside, he dropped into the passenger side of a squad car, its seats wide enough to accommodate a reptilian's wide girth. Materek settled in on his left and told the navigational unit where to go.

The car pulled away from the curb and moved slowly into a drive lane. Humans watched from the sidewalk, jeering and shouting. At a highway onramp, the car rose a few feet above the yellow lane markers and zipped along at hover-speed. Klein glanced at the steering wheel embedded in the dash and wondered if his partner knew what to do in case the auto-drive failed.

"The pod-mistress will be very upset," Materek said. "So let me ask our questions."

"Be my guest." Klein folded his arms across his chest.

"Did I tell you," Materek began, "that I may soon join a pod myself. I'm a candidate for a seventh."

"Great."

"It's an honor. The pod recently lost their seventh and many applied."

"Good luck with that." Klein sighed.

"The family we're about to visit is a pod of three. Two females and one male."

"Good to know," Klein mumbled.

"Important to know. Two females means they vie with one another to be the mistress, the leader. Very similar to your alpha male concept in your multi-person households."

Klein missed his previous partner, a human, who kept quiet on these long drives and was never eager to dig up evidence after a crime against a reptilian. But that partner's marriage broke up and he failed to find a new mate, male or female. Cops without a wife or husband, for whatever reason, were summarily dismissed from the force. As the propaganda posters said, "Marriage means stability and stability makes you practical."

The squad car dropped to the road's surface at the off ramp and cruised into a reptilian neighborhood with leafy trees, abundant bushes, and creeping vines, all of it so much different than the concrete blocks of apartment buildings in the humans' sector.

They passed cookie-cutter A-frame dwellings, many of them hidden by overgrown foliage, some with wooden fences surrounding the property. Here and there, humans trimmed hedges or mowed lawns. Others, in red prison jumpsuits, picked up trash in the streets.

The navigation screen flashed when they came to a stop. "You are at your destination," the car announced, first in the aliens' language of clicks and barks, then in English. Materek slipped out, adjusted her blue one-piece uniform, smoothing out the wrinkles in the pants legs, and fixed her belt so the buckle's edge lined up with the buttons on her chest. Klein didn't bother to look like anything more than a rumpled uniformed cop doing his duty, however much he didn't like it.

A large reptilian stood at the open door to the house. She – Klein assumed it was the female pod-mistress – looked exactly like Materek. Same flat face, a tiny semblance of a nose with two holes for nostrils. Same oval pale gray eyes, green where humans had white.

Materek addressed the mistress in their language while Klein hung back and looked around the spacious front yard. Curious neighbors stood on their lawns, watching.

"We go inside now," Materek said, and followed the pod-mistress into the dwelling.

Klein gazed up at the high ceiling, then glanced around the large room. The sleeping quarters took up one side, a single bed tucked against the slanted wall. Bins of green plants stood end to end along the other wall. Small red balls, a sweet delicacy that Klein had tried once on a dare when he was a cadet, filled a hand-crafted clay bowl on a low table in the middle of the room. A sweet and sickly odor filled the air, reminding Klein of the smell from a chocolate factory he lived near as a boy.

Two more reptilians emerged from behind a beaded curtain. One of them dropped to its haunches while the other sat on a mat, legs crossed. No one made introductions. Klein assumed the one sitting comfortably was the other female.

"You come about our lost?" the pod-mistress asked.

"Did you see any suspicious humans in the neighborhood?" Materek asked.

"There's always monkeys around here, cleaning up, maintaining the scenery."

Klein felt the mistress' eyes dig into him. He held onto her stare with his own, determined not to be intimidated. A part of him didn't blame the female for being angry. He'd be furious if some alien kidnapped his five-year-old daughter.

The questioning went on for a few more minutes. None of the three reptilians offered any insight into what had happened. They were all home, outside on the front lawn basking in the sun, when their baby, who'd been out of its egg for barely two weeks, was stolen.

The reptilian on his haunches whispered to the pod mistress, who then said, "Keva saw a stranger walking through the backyards."

"Can you describe him? Tall? Thin?"

The pod-mistress blew air from her mouth. "All these monkeys look the same to us."

"May we see the infant's quarters?" Materek asked.

At his partner's urging, Klein trooped across the room, past a curtain, and into a sun-drenched part of the house, thanks to two skylights forty feet above. An empty wooden crate full of straw sat on the floor.

"We haven't cleaned up her spot," the pod-mistress said.

A daughter, Klein thought, and wondered how these aliens distinguished one sex from another.

"We done here?" he asked Materek. "You get all you need?"

"Yes, yes," Materek said, and then exchanged a few words with the pod-mistress.

Outside, as Klein headed to the car, his partner sidled up alongside him, and said, "I am sorry you were insulted."

"Insulted?"

"She referred to your kind as monkeys."

"Yeah. I heard that." Klein shrugged. Words like that rolled off his back. "Did you get anything useful?"

"There's a back door. I assume the kidnapper entered through there while the baby slept."

"Any idea why that one guy didn't raise the alarm if there was a human wandering in the yard?"

"He probably didn't think anything of it. Your people are always in the neighborhood." Materek looked around. "We should canvas the area, speak to the neighbors."

"Now?"

"We're here, aren't we?"

Klein shrugged. There was no getting out of this. He had to do what his partner wanted. If he didn't cooperate she might report him and he'd be looking for another job. Cops who didn't work well alongside their alien counterparts didn't last long on the force.

* * *

With the only elevator out of commission, Klein trudged up several flights of stairs to his seventh floor apartment. When he reached the landing he nodded at an elderly couple resting before proceeding further, probably to the senior dorms at 25.

Inside his apartment, he pulled off his boots and hung his faux-leather jacket in the hall closet. Clumps of sand, probably from his five-year-old, littered the linoleum floor.

"Can you remind Zarella to empty her shoes after she plays outside?" he said as he walked into the living room.

Janine sat up on the couch. "Is that how you say hello?"

He dropped into the overstuffed armchair he favored.

"They saw you in lizard town," she said.

"You spying on me?" He laughed. One of his wife's friends must've been working in the reptilians' neighborhood. "It's just another kidnapping."

"They should take better care of their kids." She slipped off the couch and sashayed towards the armchair. Still supple, with graceful feline moves honed during her years as a dancer, she moved slowly, a smile on her wide face.

"So who told you?" he asked as he took his wife into his arms.

"Does it matter?"

He shrugged.

"How big a deal is this one?"

"It's not. Just some baby. But my new partner's a stickler for process. She won't let this go until … "

"A female, huh?"

"Take a look at this." He pulled an eReady from his pants front pocket and projected a small seven by seven-inch screen in mid-air. A few more taps brought up a flat 2-D picture of a bald-headed man in denim overalls.

"How'd you get that?" his wife asked.

"We spent two hours asking around. It's a composite based – "

"Asking collaborators?"

"If you recognize this guy, better warn him."

She took another look at the composite. "Don't know him." She pulled away. "How far do you think the investigation will go?"

"It stops today, if I've got any input." He felt odd saying that. Since the police department started pairing humans with aliens, things had changed. Crimes against reptilians got more attention than in the past. He just wouldn't admit that to his wife.

She'd come into his life as a demoralized 20-year-old, her mother dead and her father transported to a lunar penal colony for his part in a terrorist organization fighting against the Reptilian takeover. Eight years ago, Klein needed a wife if he wanted to keep his job after finishing cadet training, and Janine had been a comely candidate who'd studied dance and had artistic ambition. Now, she mostly danced with their daughter, having put aside her dreams when the aliens clamped down on all forms of entertainment, claiming it promulgated anti-reptilian propaganda. Any other dancing she enjoyed was with an underground social club she'd joined a year ago.

"Zarella's up from her nap," Janine said. "Careful what you say. One of her teachers said she brags about her daddy the cop keeping us safe from the lizards."

He laughed.

"Not funny. The teacher told *me*. We're lucky she didn't report her for using that word."

"Well, she doesn't hear it from me."

"Like you never use it at home."

"I'm going to take a shower before supper," he said. "At least we don't ration the water anymore."

"I'd rather do that than kowtow to – "

"Mommy. Daddy."

Zarella dashed into the living room, her long blonde hair falling across the front of her frilly white nightdress.

Klein lifted his daughter in the air, set her down, and hurried to the bathroom, anxious to peel off his jumpsuit, get under the hot water, and change into a comfortable robe. With the child awake and listening to everything he and Janine talked about, there'd be no more subversive conversation until Zarella was asleep and out of earshot.

* * *

"Good news, Larry Klein." Materek stomped across the aisle separating the reptilian side of the dayroom from the human.

Klein looked up from his coffee. Other officers on the human side traded glances that combined to land on Klein's back.

"We have a suspect."

"How'd we get a suspect?" he asked.

"Facial mapping."

"You can't do that using a composite sketch."

"We've already picked him up. He's downstairs. Basement interrogation room four. Do you want to talk to him?"

"Has anyone cleared this?"

"Why are you objecting, Larry Klein? I told you last night I'd be using facial matching. You didn't object then."

Klein detected a note of anger in his partner's voice, which went up an octave. It trembled a bit, too. Best to back off. He didn't want her filing a report accusing him of being less than cooperative with an investigation.

He stood, gulping down the last of his coffee. Out of the corner of his eye he saw humans at the vending machines watching him. He tried to give them a "What can I do" signal with a grimace and a shrug.

In the chilly basement interrogation room, Tom Cassen, the suspect, sat on a hard metal chair. Klein shivered the moment he walked in.

"Can we turn on the heat in here?" Klein asked, addressing the camera in the corner. He sat across from

Cassen. Materek remained standing, her thick arms crossed over her chest.

Chassen shifted his eyes from one cop to the other. Like the composite sketch, his facial bones were prominent and his eyes were set close together, his nose slightly hooked and his lips thin to the point of being non-existent.

Klein jumped right to the point. "What were you doing in the reptilian neighborhood?"

"I was with a crew planting bushes and trees. The lizards like their foliage thick."

"What was the name of the landscaper?" Materek asked.

"I got picked up at Hardware Plus parking lot. I don't know who the landscaper was. None of my business, that."

Klein nodded. A lot of men and women gathered at various parking lots to find day work as maids, carpenters, handymen, and gardeners.

"Why were you seen walking through backyards?" Klein asked.

"Got planting to do. Look at your footage. You'll see a guy with a hand truck loaded with small bushes. He's walking in the alley, on the other side of the fence from me."

Clever, Klein thought. Cassen knew there'd be no surveillance video to contradict him. Lizards didn't load up their neighborhood with cameras and sound capturing equipment. The nearby market had a single camera to deter theft, and that had been installed over the objections of the Neighborhood Appraisal Society, a reptilian council that sought to keep alien living spaces untainted by human ways.

"We can hold him for a couple of days," Materek remarked to Klein as they left the interrogation room.

"Three days? He can't earn a living if he's in jail. And we've no proof of anything except for a facial match from a composite sketch,"

"He admitted to being there. I say, hold him. I got some background on this guy. His wife does day work like him, usually as a maid. Maybe she was working in the neighborhood. Or working for the parents who lost the baby."

"Yeah? Maybe. Call them."

"I think we should drive over and ask them."

"Call them. No need to – "

"They don't use telephones."

Klein laughed. "Your kind have some funny ways. Look, I'll go there with you, but you go inside by yourself."

"Is your objection based on the prejudice displayed by the pod-mistress?"

He didn't want to say, "I hate the smell of the place." Instead, he shrugged and said, "You'll get more out of her. You speak her language."

* * *

Materek walked around to the driver's side of the squad car, a disgusted look on her face. Klein guessed the interview – a very short one – hadn't gone well. "They don't use human maids," she said with a nod at the reptilian house.

"Maybe the wife was working in the area," Klein offered. "I'll talk to her."

"Figured you'd want to."

"By myself." Klein pulled out his eReady and scanned the citizen registry bank. Tom Cassen's wife, Lillian, wasn't hard to find.

"You got Tom, don't you?" she said the moment Klein stepped off the elevator on the tenth floor of the apartment building. She stood at her open doorway. He guessed she had a video link to whoever hit her buzzer downstairs.

Klein didn't want to go into the apartment. He preferred to stand in the hallway while he asked his perfunctory questions. No matter what the woman said, he'd tell his partner that she had nothing to add. Her husband went out every day of the week, seven days a week, out to stand in the same parking lot looking to get picked for day work.

"I know your wife," she said.

"You a family friend?"

"I'd say so. We're all humans here, right? Gotta stick together like."

"I don't think we have enough to hold Tom for more than the usual 72 hours. So don't worry."

"I didn't think I should."

Klein walked away. As he left the building, a block square structure just like the one he lived in, twenty-five stories high with unadorned cinder block walls, he admitted to himself that he missed the little house in which he'd grown up, with its front lawn and backyard. He missed the tree-lined street where neighbors gathered in the summer and helped one another shovel snow in the winter..

These days, the only humans in such houses were government higher-ups, corporate executives, and political types helping the reptilians rule the planet.

"Anything?" Materek asked when Klein returned to the squad car.

"Nothing worth looking into. She wasn't working when her husband was in the neighborhood."

The squad car drove back to the stationhouse.

"I want to ask something of you," she said.

Klein waited.

"I've been accepted into a pod. It's an honor and I would like you to attend the ceremony when I'm inducted."

"Ceremony?"

"Yes. Similar to your marriage rites."

"Why'd you want a human at your – "

"To show my pod that we can be friends with your kind."

We're not friends, Klein thought, but he couldn't say it. "Don't know if I'm up for that."

"Think about it. Think of what it will mean to your career. I don't know of any other human who's ever witnessed any of our ceremonies."

Klein resented having one more thing to think about it. He already had hard questions for his wife.

When he got home that evening – thankfully, the elevator was running again – he skipped any preliminaries and immediately voiced his question. "Why would Tom Cassan's wife bring you up regarding this case I'm on?"

Janine set her glass of wine on the end table by the couch.

"You involved with something I don't know about?" Klein asked.

"You don't know? A great investigator like you?"

He sat on the sofa. She squirmed away, putting space between them. "Do you really belong to a dancing club?"

"Leave this alone, Larry."

"Ever kiss a lizard?"

"You got a female partner. Have you kissed her?"

"This is serious. If they put pressure on Cassen, and if you're involved and someone uses you to pressure me..." his voice trailed off.

"You don't need to know what you don't need to know."

It'll all come tumbling down, he thought. His standing on the force. His career. Janine could be packed off to a penal colony, their daughter put into foster care, and he exiled to a labor camp for re-education.

"Can I count on you to be careful?" he asked.

"Can we count on you to get Tom Cassen out of trouble?"

* * *

The smell of lavender and chocolate, pine needles and exotic flowers didn't affect Klein as badly as he expected. He wrinkled his nose, especially when he first entered, but he didn't gag.

As the only human attending Materek's marriage ritual, he felt oval reptilian eyes studying him. A few, after staring for a bit, huddled together and whispered in their bark-click-guttural language.

"Larry Klein," Materek said as she approached. "Please meet the mistress of the pod I'll be joining. Her name is Dadellia."

The mistress strode forward. She spoke in French at first but then said. "Sorry. My previous posting was in another of your planet's countries."

Klein shrugged. "That's okay."

"Please," Materek said after Dadellia walked away to chat with other reptilians. "Let me introduce you to a few of our delicious dishes. I'm sure you will like them. No meat of course."

Klein let himself be escorted to a long table covered by a woven grass matt, the intricate weave, suffused with dyes, depicted an open prairie of yellow flowers watched over by two small moons in a blue-red sky.

"Try this," Materek urged, and placed a chocolate-colored square on his plastic plate, He added several chunks of bread and some tiny bud-size grapes. The tastes, when he succumbed to his curiosity, didn't disagree with him, and he took a second helping. He munched on the food as he wandered about the large room, absorbing the various odors, wondering when the ceremony would begin.

Five aliens took their places on a straw mat on a dais at one end of the room. The invited guests, amid a cacophony of barks and clicks, gathered in groups, everyone facing the five. Another alien stood in front of those on the mats. They all looked alike, Klein mused. One was Dadellia, the pod mistress. Klein knew the other was Materek. He recognized her by the beaded necklace around her neck.

Harmonious voices filled the air. The floor vibrated from stamping feet. The aliens on the dais made speeches directed at one another. Materk turned to a cluster of reptilians standing near the mat. They lined up and she kissed them one at a time. A queue formed leading to the dais. One by one, reptilians stepped forward for Materek's kiss.

Pushed from behind, Klein staggered forward. An alien with its tongue drooping from the side of its mouth, shoved him towards Materek. The aliens clapped.

"She's honoring you with inclusion," someone said. "Don't be afraid. Don't shame yourself."

Klein sucked in a deep breath. His chest ached. His head swam. The heat in the room rose around him. Sweat drenched his underarms. An alien grabbed his wrist.

"This is important to her."

He stepped towards Materek, eyes on hers when she leaned down and said, "Thank you, Larry Klein. This means much to me and to our professional partnership."

Eyes shut, he accepted the kiss, his lips touching Materek's just briefly. He didn't feel her mouth, nor did he smell her odor. And suddenly a sense of peace flowed through him, conjuring mental pictures of carnival rides, bringing to mind the memory of barkers culling the gullible from the crowd. A steel drum band played in the background.

Memory of the past morphed into hope for the future. He envisioned a time when reptilians and humans lived side-by-side in vast tracts of identical A-frame houses. He levitated to puffy white clouds and looked down at a peaceful Earth. A sense of contentment swelled his chest.

He wandered away, confused yet happy, intoxicated by a lizard's kiss. He leaned against a wall and tasted Materek's sweet saliva still on his lips. Did she know what the kiss would do to him? Or were the reptilians oblivious to the effect they had over humans?

A more startling question suddenly came to mind. One he answered without a second thought. This explained why the cults kidnapped baby lizards.

* * *

At home, Janine offered a perfunctory, "How was the wedding?" from another room in the apartment.

"Interesting." He decided to keep what had happened secret. This was the best Sunday he'd had in a long time. He'd never felt so happy, so elated, so....

Janine emerged from the bedroom. A black one-piece draped her body, the fabric showing off her curves.

"Going to dance?" he asked.

"That's right. Dance." She checked her cell phone. "Zarella's at a sleepover, in case you forgot."

"It's not dancing, is it?"

"My ride's here."

"I want to go with you."

Janine's paled, which accented the decorative shadows encircling her eyes. "Is that a joke?"

"I know you're not dancing. It's not a dance club. You've all but admitted it."

"Since when do you care about what I do or what I'm interested in?"

"It's dangerous."

"Then why'd you want to come?" She faced him with her hands on her hips, head thrust forward. "Sometimes you just don't make any sense."

"Curiosity." Was a baby lizard's kiss as intoxicating as an adult's.

"You walk in with me and I'll be banned. I know how they are, the rest of the..." She paused.

"Cult?"

"Club," she corrected. She went to the apartment door. "My ride's here," she snapped back over her shoulder, and left the apartment.

Chuckling to himself, Klein booted his eReady and projected a small screen above the all-purpose palm-sized computer. He logged into the municipal "Blotter." A few taps brought up a log-in box and he signed into the police-only apps menu. Janine probably thought she was really smart, he thought. But not smart enough to leave her cell phone at home.

He found her, though the accuracy was within a forty-yard radius. Just out of curiosity, he tried Tom Cassen's wife's cell number and found her there as well. He imagined the two women would talk about Tom, who was still in a basement cell while Materek sought evidence linking him to the kidnapping.

The car Klein ordered took him close to a gated community on the other side of town, not far from the large tracts of A-frames where the reptilians lived.

"I can't go in," the self-drive announced when it stopped at the tall wrought iron gate. Two guards peeked out from their kiosk.

"This is good." Klein stepped out of the car, which sped away. Taking out his cell phone, he showed the guards his police credentials.

"You're not on the list. Everybody on Commander Thorpe's list has already come by."

Thorpe? The town's top cop? "I got a late invite."

"Doesn't matter. And being a cop doesn't matter, either."

Klein disliked the arrogance in the young guard's voice. "Commander Thorpe himself sent me the invitation, so I better be on that list."

This time, the guard didn't speak. He just stood leaning against the iron gate, hands in his pants pockets. Klein called Janine's cell.

"What do you want now?" she said when she answered her phone.

"I'm at the gate."

Janine gasped.

"I want in."

"You're crazy. You know whose house I'm at?"

Klein nodded, though that couldn't be conveyed by the voice-only call. "Get me added to the invite list. Now, Janine. Thorpe won't like what I'll do about being left out."

Janine disconnected the call. Klein tried to moisten his dry mouth, but the effort was fruitless. What if the top cop left him at the gate? The ecstasy of Materek's kiss would be lost forever. He couldn't kiss her again. Not in any context.

Thorpe, clad in a bright yellow robe, bare feet in satin slippers and with a thin headband around his scalp, his bald head shining, bounced from the car that brought him to the gate.

"Are you nuts?" Thorpe said.

"I want in."

Klein waited on Thorpe's response. He hadn't expected to be confronted like this. A man like Thorpe didn't need a scandal. But, a man like Thorpe had the means to silence anyone who might expose him.

"Okay, Klein." Thorpe gestured with his head, his angry eyes not relenting, but his good sense, Klein suspected, taking charge.

They rode in silence up a winding road to the hilltop houses where the town's elite lived. All collaborators, Klein reminded himself with distaste. Real lizard lovers. Distinguished executives. Government types. All of them too smart to fight the inevitable when the lizards took over.

"If you weren't Janine's husband," Thorpe began when they alighted from the stopped cart.

"I wouldn't want in if I weren't her husband," Klein said.

They walked up to the porch. It wrapped around a three-story house, a wooden structure with a slanted roof and tall windows. Inside, Klein followed his host to the basement. In a brightly lit room he saw the Cassen woman standing with Janine. He didn't recognize anyone else.

In the center, on a large table, a box of sand held a sleeping baby reptilian, its tail, which hadn't yet fallen off, tucked between its legs. Patches of scales interspersed with bare gray skin covered its entire body. Klein wondered if this reptilian might be too young to produce the same effect he felt when he kissed Materek.

Why would so many people dare to kidnap these baby lizards if the kiss had no effect?

Someone started to call out numbers. People checked small chits they held in their hands. Some raised their hands and took a place at the table, smiling, looking overjoyed.

A lottery, he realized. To get a place by the table. When he saw that Janine had won a spot, he joined her.

"You weren't picked," she said. "I don't know what you're up to, but – "

He snatched the chit out of her hand. He glanced at the red-on-white number. Forty-seven.

"This is really too much, Larry."

"Please, Jan. I need this."

The anger in her eyes dissipated. "Something happened? At that lizard's wedding?"

"I'll make it up to you."

She shook her head. "I don't know how." She stepped away from the table.

Soon, all the spots were taken. Even so, there was jostling and poking and good-natured verbal jibes. Someone with a long stick woke up the sleeping baby. It stretched its legs, then its arms. It rolled over onto its back, using the sand to scratch an itch, Klein assumed.

Then it flipped and began to crawl.

"This way," someone whispered.

"Kiss me, kiss me," others called to the baby.

The cry went up all around the table, everyone urging the infant to come to them. They all wanted the instant bliss the lizard's kiss would bestow. Everyone wanted that small moment of pleasure.

Klein was no exception, and he joined the pleading, calling out to the baby. "Kiss me, kiss me."

Hidden Talents
Lisa Timpf

Relationships. Past decisions. Career choices. As she plucked the amoeboid forms of Delia Johnson's regrets out of the air and tossed them into the bucket, Karlee Braun categorized them. *There sure are a lot of them. And they're starting to head back toward Delia.*

Karlee leaned forward and spoke to the blindfolded woman seated opposite to her. "Delia. It's important that you try to think of something happy. Remember?"

The corners of Delia's mouth twitched downward. "It's hard. I lost my job last week. I can barely make ends meet. And you want me to think about something happy?"

"Luane will help you deal with all of that." Though she knew the blindfolded Delia couldn't see her, Karlee nodded toward her long-time friend Luane Davis, out of habit. "Right now, there's likely a lot going on in your head, right? Emotions swirling around?"

Delia nodded.

"Luane's therapy will be more effective if we can help you stop thinking about your regrets. So, please, think of a happy memory. It doesn't have to be anything big. Just something you can clearly visualize, and hold onto."

"I'll—try."

"Good."

Made unwelcome once again by happy thoughts, the regrets stopped drifting toward Delia and darted around the room, seeking a new host so they could probe that person's memory for things they wished they'd done differently. Once the regrets set up residence, Karlee knew, they would stimulate relevant memories to rise to the surface so they could feed on emotion—or tears, if they could get them. It could become a dangerous loop, once started.

Fortunately, Karlee's Teflon-lined protective headgear would keep Delia's regrets from infiltrating her consciousness, and Luane was similarly equipped.

C'mon. You know you want this. Karlee waved the Teflon-lined capture container, causing the artificial tears in the bottom to slosh around. She'd adjusted her glasses to the grey-tint setting to make the regrets more visible. Now, she could see some of them swooping toward the bucket to feed.

Karlee frowned when she saw a pair of blue regrets reverse direction and head back toward Delia. *She's losing her focus again.* Karlee shot a despairing glance toward Luane.

She bit her lower lip, thinking. Clearly, Delia found it challenging to fend off so many regrets. And they had a limited amount of time to work with.

Which meant—

Moving slowly but deliberately, Karlee doffed her protective cap, placing it to the side.

Over here, suckers, she thought. A savage sense of satisfaction warred with a fear when she saw the regrets reverse direction. She braced herself as they zoomed toward her, emitting the cranberry-citrus smell she'd learned to associate with their presence.

Though she knew what was coming, Karlee couldn't help flinching when the regrets hit her. *I wish I'd never discovered my Gift.* Karlee could feel the regrets' delight as they fed on her emotion.

Time to turn the tables.

Karlee called up a childhood memory of the day she'd gotten her first dog, a terrier puppy her parents had given as an early Christmas present. The subsequent happy thoughts drove the regrets away. They hung in the air between Delia and Karlee, as though debating their next move. Karlee snagged them and tossed them into the bucket.

Reluctant to tempt fate, Karlee snugged the cap back onto her head. She noted that Luane had moved closer to Delia and was mumbling reassurance to the other woman. *Good,* Karlee thought, noting numerous regrets hovering in the air. Luane had somehow coaxed Delia into thinking happy thoughts again, leaving the regrets unhoused.

Karlee collected them quickly. When she'd snatched up the last one, she slammed the containment unit shut and toggled her glasses to restore the untinted setting. "There. That's as good as we're going to get."

Luane removed her protective cap and stashed it, waiting till Karlee had done the same.

Now it was time to deal with the blindfold. Ostensibly, it was there to help Delia focus. In reality, Luane and Karlee always blindfolded clients when they worked together. Sometimes it was easier to keep some mystery in the process than to try to explain Karlee's actions.

"You can take the blindfold off now," Luane said, her voice gentle.

Delia blinked as her eyes adjusted to the light. "I feel—better," she said. "Less sad."

"Good," Luane said.

"I should have listened to Ava. She's in my AA group." Delia's fists tightened as she watched her companions' expressions.

"Tell us," Luane said, her voice soft.

"Ava told me to keep working the Steps, instead of falling back into old habits. And I tried. But one night, I went into the *Boar and Beer Stein* for just one drink, and stayed for several. After that, it was a struggle to stay away. Things just kept getting worse, not better. And now I'm here."

"You came for help," Luane said. "That's the important thing."

"And I do feel better." Delia smiled, the first time Karlee had seen her do so since she'd come to the session. "Though I could use a break, before we get back into the therapy session.

Luane placed a bottle of water in front of Delia. "That's not a problem. Just rest here for a couple of minutes. I'll be right back."

Luane gestured toward Karlee, who followed her to the door of the treatment room.

"Thanks for the assist," Luane said. "Now that we've cleared away some of Delia's regrets, I should be able to make progress more conventionally."

"All those regrets." Karlee shook her head. "Maybe it's just the times we live in. Everyone hears about the wonderful lives of celebrities and thinks theirs should be better. If they'd made different choices. What a waste of time and energy."

Luane shrugged. "We all have regrets. And sometimes, they perform a useful function. They help us figure out what we might have done differently, for example. Help us choose better paths in the future. But in cases like Delia's, regrets can be overwhelming."

"Glad I could help," Karlee said. "It's nice to be able to use my Gift openly."

Even as she said the word, Karlee's mouth twisted in a grimace. *Gifts* was the word that scientists, and later society, had coined for oddball capabilities, like her ability to see regrets as physical manifestations. Some scientists thought that these quirks were a side-effect of the widespread mutations as humanity's genetic makeup morphed in an effort to steer a path to survival in the face of increasing environmental and societal pressures, including climate change and the ever-present threat of nuclear war.

Though there had been, as is the case with anything new, fear at first, a counter-theory growing in popularity posited the gifts as a good thing. The Gifts, scientists argued, might help humanity adapt and cope. The Gifted might help enable faster discoveries due to out-of-the-box thinking. And who knew? Today, in 2040, it was estimated was that the Gifts were present in ten percent of the population. But in the future, maybe it would ratchet higher.

These sorts of theories didn't stop many of the Ungifted, or Normals as they preferred to style themselves, from discriminating against—harassing, even—those with the Gifts.

Was it jealousy, or fear, or a little of both?

Karlee, for one, couldn't say.

Karlee couldn't deny that her Gifts helped with her job as a police detective, giving her an insight her colleagues sometimes found uncanny.

But because of the latent resentment against her kind, and yes, because of some of the comments she'd heard in the break room and cafeteria, Karlee kept her Gift under wraps at work.

On those off-hours occasions when Luane called on her to assist with cognitive behavior therapy patients, Karlee could be herself. Because Luane knew about Karlee's Gift—had known, since their university days. The ability to be open about her talent made things easier.

Luane gestured toward the treatment room door. "I'd better get back soon. I just wanted to ask—have you made a decision about applying to that new department? What was it you called it—the 13th Precinct?"

"I think I'll stay put," Karlee said.

"I just thought—" Luane hesitated, as though considering whether to continue. "I was just thinking about what you've always said. About being more open using your Gift. Wouldn't that be just the place for it?"

"It sounds good on paper, forming a division to leverage the skills of the Gifted." Karlee moved toward the window and looked out, unseeing, over the cityscape below. "But I'm afraid it will just be a way to raise our profiles. To make us more subject to the kind of abuse and harassment we saw when the Gifts were first discovered."

"True enough." Luane moved over to join her. "But if you stay where you are—"

"It's okay." Karlee shrugged. "My current partner, Desmond, doesn't know about my Gift. But we both keep our private lives to ourselves. It works."

"Well, the deadline for applications is still a few days a way, in case you change your mind."

"I doubt I will."

**

Just as Karlee was about to leave for work the next morning, Dispatch called and directed her to a scene where a body had been found. When she arrived at the narrow, paved laneway, her partner, Desmond Ellis, was already there.

"Morning, Desmond." Karlee nodded toward the lanky, brown-haired detective. "We have a case?"

"Hey, Karlee." Desmond's face, as usual, gave away nothing of his thoughts. "A dog-walker called this in." He nodded toward a woman's body lying on the cracked asphalt beside him. "Looks as though the victim's been dead for a few hours. Likely not a robbery. She still had her shoulder bag with her. Her driver's license identifies her as Ava Roy."

Karlee took a step closer to the victim. With her back against the neighboring brick building and her arms crossed in front of her, Ava might have looked comfortable were it not for the surroundings. That, and the sorrowful expression on her face.

Crouching down, Karlee sniffed the air, detecting a hint of cranberry-citrus, so faint she might have been imagining it. Karlee toggled her glasses to the grey setting. Regrets had been here, alright. Karlee saw evidence of their presence scattered on the asphalt like shards of burst balloons. Red, yellow, green, blue, pink—an unusual number of regrets surrounded the victim, all over the map in terms of theme. These, though, had all died. Starved, no doubt, after Ava's death, with no living hosts nearby.

Strange to see so many, Karlee thought. She switched her glasses back to the normal setting and sighed. It would be so much easier if she could share her findings with Desmond. But she'd made up her mind a long time ago not to tell him about her Gift.

"Coroner will need to confirm, but it looks as though Ava was on the losing end of a car-versus-pedestrian encounter," Desmond said.

Karlee straightened and glanced around. "Pretty cramped confines, in here."

"I'm guessing it happened out there." Desmond pointed toward the mouth of the alley. "There were blood droplets on the ground, leading this way. She must've come in here to lick her wounds. She'd have had a better chance of surviving if she'd stayed out on the street to flag down help."

"She may have been running from someone," Karlee said. "Came in here to look for a hiding spot, then succumbed to her injuries."

"Could be. I'll get the tech group to check out the street cam footage. Maybe we'll get a lead that way."

"I wonder where she came from?"

"There's a bar across the street from the alley. Maybe we should start there."

"Sounds good." Karlee glanced back in the direction she'd come. "Coroner's here," she said. She leaned in closer to the body once again. "We should see what the victim has in there." Karlee pointed to Ava's clenched left hand.

Desmond nodded. "Good catch."

Karlee gazed down at the body.

We'll find whoever did this to you, she thought. She didn't usually make promises like this, to the living or the dead. But she had a prickling, uneasy feeling that this case was going to be different.

***

Later that morning, Karlee slid into her seat beside Desmond and looked at the man on the other side of the table.

Their visit to the bar had been a bust—it wouldn't open until later that day—but they had lucked out. A man named Sam Jaysmith had turned himself in, just after Karlee and Desmond returned to the Precinct.

Jaysmith slumped in his chair, shoulders slumped. More of interest to Karlee was the presence of two light blue regrets circling his head.

Desmond took the lead, while Karlee jotted notes. "So, Mr. Jaysmith, you said you thought you might have hit someone with your vehicle near the *Boar and Beer Stein*. Why did you wait to report the incident?"

"I'd had a bit to drink," Sam admitted. "I felt a bump, but I thought I might have imagined it. And I saw someone running. I thought it might have been a prankster. Hit my car and run away, you know?"

Karlee raised her eyebrows. There *had* been instances of pedestrians hitting vehicles with purses, backpacks, and other objects if they felt the vehicles had been traveling too quickly. These days, people seemed to be on edge, just looking for someone or something to take out their anger on.

"And what prompted you to turn yourself in?" Desmond leaned forward.

"Last night, I was on autopilot. Got home, parked, went into the house. But this morning, I noticed the dent in the hood." Sam lowered his gaze. "And that's when I feared that I really *had* hit someone."

"Tell us what happened."

"Like I said, I felt a bump."

"You didn't see anyone?"

"I—uh—was looking at—"

"Your phone? Are you kidding me?"

"I gave someone my number while I was at the *Third Street Wine Bar*. And they texted me."

"Fine," Desmond snapped. "And then you felt a bump."

"Yes. I glanced up, and after that I saw someone headed for the alley."

"Running?"

"Yeah. Well, limping, kind of. But she moved on her own steam. I hollered out the window at her, asked her if she needed help. She made a rude hand gesture. So I figured she was okay."

"And you drove away."

Sam lowered his head. "Yes."

"Any idea what direction she came from?"

"Look, I didn't even see her coming. But it was right near the *Boar and Beer Stein*. Maybe she came out of there . . ."

"Give us a moment," Desmond said.

He left the room, and Karlee followed.

"Well? What do you think?" Desmond asked. "Was he telling the truth?"

Karlee gathered her thoughts. Sam's regret, both about the accident and the delay in reporting it, had been there to see. Well, for her at least. And it wasn't something you could fake.

So yes, she thought he was telling the truth. But how to convey that to Desmond, convincingly, without giving away how she knew?

Fortunately, she'd had lots of time to practice that particular form of evasiveness.

"He's clearly at fault, by his own admission," Karlee said. "He wasn't watching the road. And we'll have to check for any connection between Ava and Sam, just to confirm this wasn't pre-meditated. But I believe Sam when he says he didn't do it on purpose. And if he wished Ava harm, wouldn't he have followed her into the alley to finish the job?"

A tall, lean man walked toward Karlee, leaning slightly forward as he approached with hurried strides. "Excuse me, Detectives, there's something you need to see."

"Hey, Finn," Desmond said. Karlee, too, nodded a greeting to the tech expert.

Finn flourished his tablet. "We pulled this off the street-cam near the scene." He toggled the screen of his device. Karlee looked over Desmond's shoulder as a video began to play.

Just as a silver SUV edged into the picture, Ava Roy emerged from a pool of shadow beside the *Boar and Beer Stein*. She stumbled, moving awkwardly, as though she'd been pushed. Her momentum carried her into the path of the approaching vehicle.

After the impact, Ava pivoted, then staggered across the street. She fired a backward glance, not at the vehicle, as Karlee might have expected, but toward the pool of shadow. Ava waved her hand in a defiant gesture, then disappeared into the alley.

"So. It seems Sam Jaysmith was telling the truth," Desmond said. He nodded to Karlee. "Like you said, though, we'll check for a connection a connection between them. Now we need to figure out why she came out of the shadows so quickly." He turned to face Finn. "Does the video show anyone coming out of that area afterwards?"

"Unfortunately, no," the video tech said. "That's all I've got."

"It's helpful, thanks," Desmond said. "We'll wait for the coroner's report, but it seems likely that the impact with Sam Jaysmith's car killed Ava. Without a push, though, it's unlikely she would have ended up in harm's way. Now we need to find someone with motive to hurt Ava Roy."

Karlee checked her wrist chrono. "Well, the *Boar and Beer Stein* should be open by now."

Desmond's jaw took on a grim set. "Let's make that our next stop. As soon as we finish processing Mr. Jaysmith."

***

Karlee had never been inside the *Boar and Beer Stein*, but on first glance, it seemed typical of establishments of its sort: dark wood, brown leatherette booths whose tattered fabric had seen better days, and the smell of spilled beer and greasy fries heavy in the air despite the early hour. Large television screens hung on the walls, tuned to an assortment of sports events. The handful of patrons took little interest. Their faces bore the same sorrowful expressions as Ava Roy's.

Only the bartender and wait staff, clad in teal T-shirts with matching caps bearing the bar's insignia, appeared immune to the general air of sadness.

"Was this woman here last night?" Desmond toggled his phone, then showed Ava's photo to bartender Logan Williams.

"Yeah, I saw her." Logan frowned. "She asked for a cola, and sat at the bar like she was waiting for someone."

"She seem upset or anything?" Desmond asked.

"She had a tiff with a man who was in here."

"Were they together?"

"They arrived at different times. But they started to argue, and left together." The bartender shot a nervous glance toward the far corner of the room.

"Can you describe the man?"

"He was tall—about my height. Blond hair. Looked like he was in good shape. Now, if you don't mind, I have patrons to attend to." He shot another glance to the back corner.

Karlee caught a glimpse of a broad-shouldered man wearing a *Boar and Beer Stein* T-shirt and cap. The man rose to his feet, then headed for a door marked "Staff Only."

Wow, he sure looks like Calvin, Karlee thought.

Same height, same rigid posture . . .

But what would Calvin Gagnon be doing in Baytown? She hadn't seen him in what, a dozen years? And that had been at Gwillham University, miles from here . . . Karlee shook her head. "Who was that? Back there?" She fixed her gaze on Logan.

"Where?"

"You kept looking back to that corner," Karlee said, stabbing a finger in the direction of the spot where she'd seen the mystery man. "I want to know why."

Logan's shoulders sagged. "That was Johnny. He owns the place. I was trying to figure out how to get rid of you guys so I could get back to work. Johnny's always on us about wasting time."

Johnny. So it wasn't him. Karlee felt a surge of relief.

She looked at Desmond, and frowned. Her partner's face looked drawn, and beads of sweat showed on his forehead. He shifted his weight, as though anxious to be quit of the place. Karlee understood the feeling. The longer they stayed here, the more uneasy she felt.

But why?

Karlee turned away and toggled her glasses, activating the grey tint feature. This time, when she looked around the room, she saw schools of regrets drifting through the air. Now and then, a few would peel off from the group to dip down toward one of the patrons, though they showed no interest in the wait staff or the bartender.

Karlee flared her nostrils. Underlying the stale-beer smell, she detected a familiar cranberry-citrus tang. She tensed as a thought hit her.

I don't have my protective cap with me.

A red ameboid form zoomed toward her. Certain that her usual actions would stand out in a place like this, Karlee suppressed the impulse to swat it away.

Two more regrets floated toward Karlee.

How could I not have realized that Zippy was terminally ill and not just off her food? I should have treasured those last few weeks with her...

Karlee put her hand on the back of a nearby chair. She felt so tired. Maybe she should just take a break. Sit here awhile. Have a beer, maybe two.

No! She shook her head. *Happy. Think of something happy, like you always tell people to.*

With an effort, Karlee fended off the regrets that had besieged her. Driven away by Karlee's happy memories, the regrets that had swarmed her drifted off in search of easier prey. But Karlee still felt troubled. The bar was saturated with regrets. More than there should have been for a crowd this size.

And she'd seen that phenomenon before.

Karlee studied the Staff Only door, longing to burst through and demand answers.

Instead, she stayed put. She couldn't press the issue now. Not without more information. A look at Desmond, who stared at a TV screen with his shoulders rounded and the corners of his lips quirked downward, confirmed that her companion was in no shape to back her up.

Karlee leaned forward. "Let's get out of here," she said.

Moving more slowly than usual, Desmond turned to face her. "Pardon?"

"Let's go." Karlee took Desmond's elbow and steered him toward the door.

***

Once he'd stumbled out of the bar and into the fresh air, Desmond turned his face up toward the sky and drew several deep breaths. Then he glared at Karlee. "Why the rush? I was just about to order a beer and settle in."

"Think about it," Karlee said. "We're both on duty."

"Oh. Yeah." Desmond's eyes had a faraway dreaminess she recognized.

"Think of something happy," she said.

"Like drinking my favorite beer?"

"If that makes you happy."

Desmond cocked his head. "What's this all about?"

Karlee hesitated. In many of the cases they'd worked together, her ability to see regrets had proven handy, though it hadn't been central to the investigation.

In the Ava Roy case, she had a feeling that regrets played a critical role, in a way she couldn't yet put her finger on. And if she didn't say anything—

There was no decision, really, she thought, shaking her head. She'd sworn to uphold the law. And withholding something that could help them on a case—

"I'm going to tell you something in confidence," she said. "But for reasons you'll soon understand, it's not something I want spread around the Precinct."

"Okay, shoot," Desmond said.

They walked back to the unmarked police car. And Karlee told him about her Gift.

***

When Karlee had finished, Desmond smiled. "Is that all?"

"It's not going to make a difference, is it, in the way we work together?"

"Why would it?" Desmond studied her face for a moment, then shook his head. "No, that's not fair. I understand your hesitancy, but I can assure you, it's not a problem for me."

They both fell silent.

Karlee couldn't help thinking about the incidents of harassment that had occurred when the Gifted were first discovered. She suspected Desmond had the same thing on his mind.

"I'll keep your secret for now, but I think there may come a day when you don't object to sharing it more widely," Desmond said.

Karlee gave him a sharp look.

"I'd give you the reason, but it's not my story to tell," he said. "Now, I'm assuming the reason you shared this is because it pertains to the case?"

"It is," Karlee said. "That bar was loaded with regrets. I saw them."

Desmond frowned. "What bar isn't?"

"No, an abnormal amount."

"So? A lot of people go there to drown their sorrows."

"It's more than that. It's as though somebody put them there on purpose."

"Huh." Desmond mulled it over for a moment. "The more the patrons drink, and the harder the regrets hit them. And the more burdened by regrets they get, the more they feel the need for another drink. It's underhanded, if someone's doing that deliberately, but there's no law against it."

"Maybe so," Karlee said. "But I can't help thinking this could be connected to what happened to Ava."

"Well, thanks for sharing that with me," Desmond replied. "Let's head back to the Precinct. I'll call ahead and see if Finn can figure out who our mystery man is."

"The guy Logan mentioned?"

"Yeah. Maybe he can shed some light on things."

***

By the time Karlee and Desmond arrived at the Precinct, Finn Hayes had already identified a person of interest. He walked over and angled the screen of his tablet so the other two could see the image of a blond man.

"He fits the bartender's description," Desmond conceded. "Then again, so could a lot of guys I know."

"There's plenty of photos of him on Ava Roy's social media, up till about two months ago," Finn said. "Meet Brock Tremblay, Ava's ex-boyfriend."

"A heated argument, and maybe some residual bad feelings. Wouldn't be the first time that proved to be the recipe for trouble," Desmond mused.

"That's for sure," Karlee said. And she could think of one particular instance where that had, regrettably, been true.

***

Brock Tremblay's knuckles whitened. "I don't know how many times I have to tell you. I wouldn't do anything to hurt Ava."

Karlee, sitting beside Desmond with her glasses toggled to the grey tint setting, studied the suspect. Brock oozed regret, but not for a violent act, which would have shown up in reds and oranges. No, his regrets were muted. Lavender and various shades of blue, suggesting a quieter sentiment. Regret for the way things turned out, perhaps. Regret for all the little things said, or not said. Actions, or inactions, that were easier to see after the fact than in the heat of the moment.

"The bartender at the *Boar and Beer Stein* says you argued with Ava," Desmond said.

"We had a discussion. I knew how badly she wanted to quit drinking, so I didn't understand why she was in there. Why she'd subject herself to temptation."

"You broke up a couple of weeks ago, right? Why the interest in what she was doing?"

"I still care about her."

"Maybe you care about the money you owe her, too." Desmond put a piece of paper on the table. "We found this exchange in Ava's email. Says here you owed her two grand."

"I borrowed some money off her last month. To pay some bills."

"Gambling debts, more like."

Brock hung his head. "Yeah. Losing that money is what made me finally hit rock bottom. I swore off gambling after that. Set up a payment plan, which I planned to follow to the letter."

"Maybe you found it tempting to get rid of her. Push her in front of a car, and any memory of what you owed her would die with her."

"I told you. I wouldn't hurt her," Brock said. "Besides, I left the bar before she did. I'd said my piece. It was clear she didn't want to listen. And I couldn't sit there and watch her spiral down again."

Desmond checked his notes. "You left before her?"

"Yeah. Then I walked back home. I live a few blocks from here."

"Can anybody vouch for you?"

"Our building has a surveillance system in the lobby. You're welcome to check."

***

"Well? What did you think?" Desmond asked, once they'd left the interview room.

Karlee hesitated. "I know Brock seems like our best lead. But I have a sense he was telling the truth. His regret seemed genuine. And you can't fake that."

Karlee was surprised by the relief she felt at being able to state openly what she'd so often had to keep silent. *Maybe telling Desmond about my Gift will work out after all.*

"If it wasn't Brock, that would leave us back at square one." Desmond sighed. "It feels as though we might have hit a dead end."

Karlee thought about the promise she'd made to Ava. There had to be a way to crack this case. But what?

"What did the coroner's report reveal?" Karlee asked.

"Ava's tox screen showed no signs of drugs or alcohol. And the coroner confirmed the vehicle impact to be the cause of death."

Karlee shook her head. *So much for that . . .* "Did she send photos?"

"Yeah. But there was nothing unusual that I could see. I'll show you."

Karlee studied Desmond's computer screen as he flipped through the images. When he got to one with Ava lying on the exam table with her hands at her sides, palms upward, Karlee asked him to stop. On impulse, she toggled her glasses.

"There," she said, pointing.

"There, what?" Desmond raised his eyebrows.

"Sorry. Forgot you can't see them." Karlee adjusted the tint on her glasses and frowned. "I'm not sure whether it's significant, but I can see the shards of several regrets in the palm of Ava's right hand."

"Why would she have regrets in her *hand*?" Desmond turned his own hands palm-upward. "Do *I* have regrets in my hand?"

"No. You don't. To have as many as she has, you'd have to grab them on purpose." Karlee paused. "What if Ava had the same Gift as me? What if she found out what the *Boar and Beer Stein* was up to? And confronted someone about it?"

"If she threatened to blow the whistle, that would be motive." Desmond scowled. "If you're right, the bartender misled us."

"He did keep looking into the back corner of the room. Like he was worried about whoever was back there." On a hunch, Karlee toggled her comm device, looking for information about the *Boar and Beer Stein*. The bar had been purchased two months ago by a man named Johnny Gagnon.

Karlee drew in a sharp breath when she saw a publicity photo taken at the grand re-opening. *That's Calvin.*

"The new owner is somebody I knew from university." She gritted her teeth before continuing. "His full name was Calvin John Gagnon. It seems he goes by Johnny now."

"How does that help us?"

"He did the something similar when we were at university. Weaponizing regrets, that is. And if Ava threatened to expose him, I could see him reacting strongly . . ."

That, Karlee knew, was an understatement.

"It's not much to confront him with. We'll need evidence."

Karlee paused. She'd hoped to never see Calvin again. But if they wanted to solve this case, she'd have to suck it up. For Ava's sake. "If you set me up with a wire, I can try to get a confession out of him. But I'll need you standing by, as backup."

"I can do that," Desmond said. "But what makes you think he'll confess to you?"

"We have a history. Let's meet at the *Boar and Beer Stein* in two hours. There's a couple of things I need to do, first. One of which is to fab up some protective headgear for you."

***

Karlee's first stop was her own residence. She hurried into the laundry room and opened the bucket carrying Delia Johnson's regrets. Normally, she just let them starve, and it appeared a number of them had done just that. But luckily, she could spot a few survivors, sustained by the artificial tears at the bottom of the container.

Good. Karlee grabbed a smaller container and, working carefully, put several of the still-living regrets inside, then snapped the lid shut.

Now, to fab up Desmond's headgear. As she worked on lining her partner's Baytown Police Department baseball cap with a protective coating, Karlee's mind drifted back to Calvin.

Calvin had been the first person to help Karlee understand her Gift. She'd seen him around in her Introductory Humanities class. Calvin was hard to miss. Broad-shouldered, red-haired, and possessed of a slightly arrogant air, he wasn't the sort of person to whom Karlee would have naturally been drawn. But fate had thrown them together in a group project. One evening when they'd met to discuss the project, Calvin lingered behind after the others left.

"I saw you watching Edra." Calvin grinned, flashing white teeth. "Did you notice anything?"

Karlee looked down, wondering how to respond. Nobody had asked her a question like that before. Knowledge about the Gifts was just starting to come out, and there remained a lot of prejudice against the Gifted. Did she want to expose herself? With someone she barely knew?

"I'm guessing you noticed the same thing I did." Calvin cocked his head. "Regrets, swirling around her head."

"Is that what they are?" A wave of relief prompted Karlee to abandon her hesitancy. *What if he was having me on?* She studied Calvin's expression.

But rather than being taunting, as she'd feared, his smile was one of encouragement. "Here. Try these." Calvin handed her a pair of grey sunglasses.

Karlee put the glasses on, then looked at the chair where Edra had been sitting. The grey tint made the vague forms she sometimes saw with the unaided eye as blurs pop out with greater clarity. "So they really are there," she said. "I was afraid there was something wrong with my eyes. Or that I was seeing ghosts or something."

"What you're seeing is physical manifestations of regrets. You're one of the Gifted."

Calvin made that proclamation as though it were a big deal, but instead of elation, Karlee felt a stab of fear. "What if I don't want to be able to see them?"

"Don't say that!" Calvin leaned forward. "Think of it as something special. Something that sets you apart. Sets us apart."

"I don't even see the point of it."

"I don't quite know how to capitalize on it, either." Calvin's expression assumed a far-away look. "Not yet. But I'm confident I will."

Drawn together by mutual interests uncovered during their group project, and by the Gift they shared but couldn't talk about to others, Karlee and Calvin began to hang out together. Sometimes they met up for a beer at the Lower Level Pub on campus. Other times, they went to the music room in Karlee's residence for a jam session, with Calvin on piano and Karlee playing her guitar.

But Karlee spent time with other friends, too. After a couple of months had passed, Calvin started exhibiting jealousy.

"I have a lot of interests," Karlee told him.

Calvin moped for a moment. "Don't you see? We need to stick together."

"No. I don't see. I'm still *me*, despite my Gift. My friends will understand that."

"Will they?"

Karlee didn't like the sly look that accompanied that remark. "What do you mean by that?"

"Lots of people think of the Gifted as freaks. We're better off sticking together."

"Why do you say that?"

"I'm just preparing myself."

"Calvin, nothing says we can't use our Gifts for the good."

Calvin shrugged. "We were given them for an evolutionary reason. That's what the scientists say, isn't it? It must mean we're supposed to be in charge."

"It may not mean that at all," Karlee said. "Look, I've got to go. Talk later?"

***

The talk came sooner than Karlee expected, and under different circumstances.

Karlee had joined up with Luane and some of the other members of the women's ice hockey team at the Lower Level Pub. The group had just started doling out their second pitcher of beer when Calvin arrived.

Karlee stood up. "Hey, Calvin."

Calvin jerked his head to invite her to a private conversation, off to the side. He pulled out a chair at a table nearby and sat down, dropping his gym bag, zipper open, on the floor beside him.

"What are you doing here?" Karlee tried to keep an edge from her voice.

"I wanted to show you the truth about the people you're hanging around with."

"What's that supposed to mean?"

Calvin tugged his baseball cap lower. A muscle twitched in his cheek. "You need to choose which side you're on. The weak, or the strong."

Karlee just started at him.

"I'll bet your *friends* can't handle regrets," Calvin sneered. "Watch."

"Watch—what?" Karlee fumbled for the pair of grey-tinted sunglasses she'd purchased after trying Calvin's. She spotted a cloud of regrets drifting toward her friends' table. "Where did they come from?"

Calvin nodded toward the open bag. "I've been collecting. Ready for some fun?"

"Fun? You think this is a joke?" Karlee stood up quickly, causing the feet of her chair to scrape across the floor. She shot a look at her friends. "You say I need to choose?" Karlee stabbed a finger toward Luane. "I choose them. Now get out of here. I never want to see you again."

Calvin looked stunned, but just for a moment. With quiet dignity that almost, but not quite, disguised his bruised emotions, he rose to his feet, zipped the gym bag shut, and headed for the door.

Karlee hurried over to join Luane and the others.

"That paper I left to the last minute. Why did I do that?" Luane turned to Karlee, her face tear-streaked. "Not working out as much as I should. Taking psych as my option course instead of calculus. I'm good at math, you know."

"I know." Karlee patted her friend's arm. "Come to think of it, I wish I'd tried out for the volleyball team, first year. It was my best sport in high school." She drew a deep breath. The cranberry-citrus smell that she was just learning to associate with regrets permeated the area. "Listen up, everyone," she said. "Try to think of something happy."

The team's first-line centre, Tina, gave her a blank-eyed stare. "Hap-py?"

"Yes. Happy. Like—uh—you got an A on your midterm, didn't you?"

"Huh. I guess I did." Tina's face creased in a grin.

It took some time, but gradually Karlee's friends regained their good mood. But she didn't forgive Calvin for what he'd done.

After that night, Karlee had steered clear of Calvin. Now, as she put the finishing touches on Desmond's protective cap, she wondered whether cutting ties had been the right thing to do. Maybe, back at university, there was a time when Calvin might have been turned to a different path. Maybe she should have tried harder to remain friends.

What's done is done, she told herself. *The only thing we can influence is the future.*

She didn't find that thought as comforting as she might have liked.

***

Karlee parked down the street from the *Boar and Beer Stein*, still haunted by memories of the past. She shook her head. Funny, how the memory of events that had happened so long ago still resonated with such intensity. Like echoes through time, or ripples caused by a rock thrown into a still pond. Because if she was right, they were still feeling the ripples of Calvin's actions.

At the agreed-upon time, she climbed into the Baytown Police Force's audio surveillance van. She handed Desmond his modified headgear, and tugged her own Teflon-lined baseball cap, fitting it securely.

Karlee battled a surge of nervous tension as the female tech equipped her with the audio and visual surveillance devices. "All set," the woman said. She stepped back.

"I'll be ready to back you up," Desmond said.

"Good," Karlee said, pleased to note that her voice betrayed no sign of her nervousness.

Once inside the *Boar and Beer Stein*, Karlee took a moment to let her eyes to adjust to the gloom. Spotting Logan Williams behind the bar, she sidled over. "I have a feeling you held some information back about the night Ava Roy died."

"Ava Roy? Who's that?"

"The woman whose photo we showed you, last time we were in here." Karlee leaned forward. "Look, unless you want us to start poking around—"

"Fine," he snapped. "She had an argument—a confrontation—with Johnny. But I didn't hear what they were talking about. After they started talking, he took her to his office."

"Which is—?" Karlee raised her eyebrows.

"That way."

As she made her way toward the office, Karlee tried to suppress her elation. So, Ava *had* argued with Calvin. Which meant their theory just might be right . . .

When Karlee got to Calvin's office, she found the door unlocked. She knocked, then entered.

A bareheaded Calvin looked up from his laptop. Karlee glanced around, noting that he'd left his protective cap on a hook near the door. *Good.*

"Karlee Braun. What a pleasant surprise." Calvin's facial expression belied his words. "Close the door, will you?"

Karlee complied. "Nice to see you, too. I'm here about Ava Roy."

"Who?"

"The woman who confronted you about your little scheme. Making people wallow in regrets so they drop more cash in your bar."

"It's not illegal."

He didn't deny it. "Only because the law hasn't yet caught up to those of us with the Gifts." Karlee frowned. "Infecting people with regrets might not be against the law, but pushing someone in the path of a moving car is. What happened? Did Ava threaten to go public?"

"She wanted me to refuse service to her friend Delia, and any other Alcoholics Anonymous members who stepped across our threshold. She said if I didn't, she'd out me."

"Would that have been so bad?"

Calvin crossed his arms, his expression wary. "Why should I tell you anything?"

Time for Plan B.

Karlee put her right hand in her pocket and popped open the lid of the small jar inside. "You always said you despised people who couldn't handle regrets."

"They're weak," he said. "Face it, the Gifted will one day rule the world. We're all superior in some way to the rest of the rabble. In fact, if you were to join me here, we could make a real killing. Open another bar, across town—"

"I don't want to use my Gifts against other people. I want to use it to help them."

"Then you're naïve." Calvin turned away, so she wouldn't see his facial expression. "We need to be on the defensive. People would reject us, if they knew."

"Calvin, it doesn't have to be like that. People know about me, and they don't reject me."

"Oh, so you're completely open about who you are, at work, are you?"

"Not completely, but—"

"Don't you remember that night, when we watched the news together? When the flash mob attacked the small group of the Gifted, on the main street of Gwillham?"

Karlee closed her eyes. Of course, she remembered. Who among the Gifted would ever forget the visceral fear that arose from witnessing what people were capable of, at their worst? She drew a deep breath, searching for calm, with limited success. "That was at the start. When people didn't know much about us. Calvin, I'm not excusing it, but people were afraid."

"They're *still* scared, most of them. Don't you get that? They're just too smart to admit it. Yes, people have learned since that first incident, when the law came down hard. They know better than to be open about their distrust. But it's still there. Which is why we always need to strike first." Calvin looked around the room, his eyes wide. His voice dropped to a whisper. "What did you do?"

"I struck first." Karlee flourished the now-empty jar. "I let some of our friends out to play."

Anticipating Calvin's next move, Karlee grabbed his teal *Boar and Beer Stein* cap off the hook and had a quick look. *Teflon-lined. Like I suspected.* She threw the cap into the far corner of the room. With her other hand, she toggled her glasses.

Calvin lurched forward. "Just—let me get that, will you? Maybe we can work something out."

"You'll get the hat. Once you make a full confession." Karlee ducked involuntarily as a blue regret zooming toward her. The regret bounced off her cap, emitting the familiar cranberry-citrus scent. It hovered for a moment, as though stunned, then zoomed toward Calvin.

With a pained expression, Calvin batted at the air.

Good. They're taking effect, Karlee thought.

Calvin moaned and put his head in his hands. His shoulders shuddered and Karlee saw moisture on his face. "Get rid of them. And I'll talk."

Karlee hesitated. Was this a ruse?

But when Calvin raised his head to look at her, his expression vulnerable, she caught a glimpse of the friend she'd once had.

Moving quickly, Karlee snatched up the regrets circling Calvin's head and stuffed them into the container. When she'd finished the task, she snapped, "Fine. Now spill."

Calvin hesitated. Fearing he might renege on his promise, Karlee waved the jar at him.

With his gaze fixed on the container, Calvin began talking. "Okay. You're right, I had a sweet deal going, and Ava was threatening to wreck it. So I followed her out the side door, and we argued. She tried to get past me, to go back into the bar. Threatened to shout out the truth right then and there. I lost my temper, and I shoved her away." He shook his head. "I *do* regret that. I didn't mean to push her so hard. She lost her balance and staggered onto the road. And then—"

"Then Sam Jaysmith came along." Karlee nodded. It fit. "You tried to cover it up. The bartender's story, about an argument between Ava and her ex-boyfriend—I'm sure you told him what to say."

"*That* argument did happen. But yeah, I told Logan to change the time line, to cast suspicion."

Hearing a noise behind her, Karlee turned toward the door. Desmond shouldered through the entry-way, the protective cap that Karlee had prepared for him firmly in place.

"I heard it all." Desmond tapped his earpiece. "We've got enough to go on. Good work." And the warm, welcoming smile that accompanied that comment provided Karlee all the confirmation she needed that Calvin had been wrong about the need to keep silent about her Gift, for fear of rejection.

***

"Thanks for the backup," Karlee said, once they'd returned to the Precinct. She lowered her voice. "And for the support."

"I just wish you'd told me sooner," Desmond said. "Though I understand why you didn't."

"I couldn't take the risk."

"Then I'll take one." Desmond sighed, then continued. "Look, don't take this the wrong way, but I think you should apply for a job at the new Precinct."

So that's the way it's going to be? Karlee narrowed her eyes. "You don't want to work with me now, is that it?"

"That's *not* it," Desmond said. "Truth is, I suspected you had a Gift. The uncanny way you seemed to come up with clues to help us solve cases—I always thought your gift was enhanced intuition, or something like that."

"If you suspected, then what about the others?" Karlee shot a panicked look around the squad room.

"I doubt it," Desmond said. "There's a reason I'm more attuned to it. My older sister has a Gift as well."

"Oh."

"She swore me to secrecy, though I don't think she'd begrudge me telling you. And it's been hard, in the squad room, hearing some of the things people say." Desmond's hands closed into fists.

"Why are you suggesting I apply elsewhere?" Try as she might, Karlee couldn't keep a note of suspicion from her voice.

"Because at the new Precinct, they're planning to truly leverage the skills of the Gifted," Desmond said. "You'd be working on important cases, including situations where criminals are using their Gifts to commit crimes. Understandably, the bulk of the rank and file aren't equipped for cracking those sorts of cases."

"Checks and balances," Karlee said.

"Something like that." Desmond paused, as though choosing his words carefully. "Look, if you want to stay, I'll keep your secret. I'll gladly work with you. If anything, knowing about your Gift will improve our working relationship."

Karlee mulled it over. Isn't this new relationship with Desmond what she'd wanted? To be able to work the way she had with Luane? To be open about who she was, with those she was most closely affiliated to?

But her encounter with Calvin had shown that some of the Gifted were, in fact, using their talents to their own advantage. Desmond was right. The best way to make a difference, if she truly wanted that, would be working in a group where her talents could be utilized to the fullest.

"There's no guarantee I'll get in," she said.

"I'll put in a good word, if that would help."

"I'd appreciate it."

She checked her wrist chrono. "Quitting time, already." And as she headed for the door, Karlee couldn't help feeling excited. To be able to be herself, openly—it was a possibility she hadn't allowed herself to contemplate, until now.

Desmond felt into step beside her. "Celebratory drink? On closing the case?"

"One drink. And then I have something I need to do." Karlee grinned. "I've got an application to fill out. And the sooner I get started, the better."

The Astronaut Always Rings Twice
Edited by Shannon Allen and JR Campbell
Tyche Books Ltd., August 2022
Reviewed by Lisa Timpf

Hot chocolate and marshmallows. Peanut butter and jam. Ham and cheese. Allowing some variability for personal taste, some foods just seem to pair up nicely. But what happens when you blend genres instead of gustatory delights? Would a mash-up of noir detective stories and science fiction would make for a tasty combination? Reading *The Astronaut Always Rings Twice*, a short story collection blending dark detectives and dark matter, gave me a chance to decide for myself.

Edited by Shannon Allen and JR Campbell and published by Tyche Books Ltd., *The Astronaut Always Rings Twice* serves up 15 stories. The table of contents hints that the stories will, in true noir tradition, expose society's darker underbelly. Titles like "Where the Devil Can't Go," "The Diary of a Dead Diplomat," and "Mary Kaye Will Always Break Your Heart" both spark curiosity and foreshadow what lies ahead.

The science fiction slant of the stories plays out in the attributes of the detectives and their partners, in the settings, and in the crimes themselves. Crimes to be solved include the murder of a synthetic, the race to find a hacker before they destroy society, and the death of an alien diplomat. Some of the detectives sport cybernetic enhancements. One is a character from virtual reality who has morphed into a physical body, and another solves his assigned case as an avatar while his body rests in suspended animation. Detectives' partners and sidekicks include aliens, AIs, and cyborgs. As for the settings, the authors whisk us off to dystopian societies on future Earth, Mars, space stations, a data-mining moon, and a giant starship.

When it comes to imagining what the future might look like, the authors' creativity really shines. In "The Flowers of Spring" by Michael Teasdale, after the

"Android Spring," the Luddites have taken charge, and synthetic life forms that were once accorded respect are now second-class citizens. "Jurisdiction" by Al Onia is set in a society physically separated according to socio-economic class, and transitions between the levels of "Midton," "The Heights," and "The Pinnacle," are guarded as jealously as the borders between countries. In "BronzeShield Plus" by Douglas DiCicco, the level of policing coverage is based on the policy a given municipality or jurisdiction has purchased from Justice Solutions. In the case of Carl Zeal, the Investigative Technician assigned to unearth the facts behind a young man's murder, resources and time allocated to solve the crime are limited by the fact that the ward where the murder occurred had opted for budget-level coverage.

Each of the stories had its appeal, and from a science fiction lover's viewpoint, *The Astronaut Always Rings Twice* hit the mark. But what about the noir side of things?

My reading and viewing interests have, for a long time, included detective stories, mysteries, and police procedurals, but I will freely confess that I haven't had much exposure to noir fiction. I was intrigued by the prospect of noir detective stories that took a science fiction slant, but not certain what to expect.

In the book's foreword, co-editor Shannon Allen states, "Science fiction gives us the possibilities. Noir exposes our darkest corners." There certainly is darkness in *The Astronaut Always Rings Twice*. The stories doesn't always end with the crime solved and loose ends neatly tied up. The protagonists are battling against systems that often seem to be working against them. The physical surroundings are, in many cases, grim. In some instances, detectives take on a case knowing from the outset that the prospects of solving it are slim to nil, but they plod on anyway.

That doesn't mean that *The Astronaut Always Rings Twice* is a total gloom-fest. Offsetting the darkness is an undercurrent of humor, albeit often cynical, running through the stories. In "The Flowers of Spring," the detective Drake describes his initial survey of the crime scene: "I shuffle over to the corpse and crouch down, knees popping like distant gunshots. These days my whole body feels like a perp resisting arrest." In "Twelve Days of Christmas" by Chris Barnham, detective Hammett encounters a librarian "wearing an antique wool two-piece and hair pulled up into a bun so severe it looked like it would slap your wrist for making a noise." The humor provides a counter-point to the darkness. Snappy dialogue, a feature of many noir detective stories, keeps things moving and adds laughs as well.

When it comes to foreboding descriptions, the authors in the collection don't disappoint. In "The Diary of a Dead Diplomat" by Ewan A. Dougall, "rotting piles of garbage climb the walls like fetid vines." In "The Flowers of Spring," "the crackle of the neon signs above are a music only residents of this scum-filled city could learn to love." In "BronzeShield Plus," Investigative Technician Carl Zeal walks through the rain, but not just any rain: "PureRain, contrary to what the brand name implied, contained numerous chemical pesticides and synthetic nutrients, intended to promote growth in the rooftop agricultural projects."

It's difficult, and probably unfair, to pick out individual stories for the spotlight. I found the quality of the collection even, with each of the stories having its strengths. Nonetheless, I will give a few special mention. I'd previously encountered Michael Teasdale's writing in *Trenchcoats, Towers, and Trolls: Cyberpunk Fairy Tales*, published by World Weaver Press, and enjoyed the powerful descriptions, the humor, and the sense of that the story extended beyond the margins. Teasdale uses some distinct wording, like "peeped" instead of saw or perceived, just frequently enough to give his stories a unique flavor without overdoing it.

In "Mary Kaye Will Always Break Your Heart," J.W. Schnarr creates a tale about trying to recover a 2003 Fender 'Mary Kaye' Stratocaster guitar, weaving in music history with dystopia in a story that blends fact and futuristic fiction. "The Inseparable Fun Boys" by

Wendy N. Wagner takes us to New Angeles, "Mars' brightest town, its loudest town, a wild party town that had come to fill its entire atmodome." "The Inseparable Fun Boys," like many of the other stories, features a protagonist caught up in nostalgia and in this case, gives readers a deeper resonance with *Alice in Wonderland* references.

Back to my original question: do the noir detective and science fiction genres make a tasty blend? If you enjoy dark humor, flawed heroes doggedly working their cases even when the odds seem to be stacked against them, and strange, often dystopian, twists on society, the answer is a resounding "yes."

Content Warning (which may contain spoilers, and may not be all-inclusive): As one might expect given the "noir" aspect, several of the stories deal with dark issues, including murder and kidnapping. Most of the descriptions of physical violence didn't bother me, but one accident scene was disquieting as much for the indifference of the perpetrator as for the damage done to the victims. There was also a story that described victims who had been physically mutilated. This was disturbing for me, though it may not be an issue for all readers.

Customer Satisfaction
Rosie Oliver

The evening has gone quiet in the Romulisa café with the rush hour over. The last few stragglers sip their drinks, waiting for whatever. Samanda sends Atsuo to clean the empty tables while she deals with behind the counter chores, the most urgent being to order fresh supplies. She opens her till account. A purple tag, hex shade 7851a9, flashes over her inbox icon. An angel AI, who helps people through depression, stress, anger management and self-loathing, has left a message.

Not again. What is going to go wrong now? The last and only time had been a nightmare. She cannot go through that kind of thing again: being wrongly charged with a murder, and losing her fiancé and many so-called friends. Urielle, her angel AI, had to find programming workarounds to function beyond what they are allowed to do to get her out of that mess. The angel has stayed silent since. Could this be her, or is it one of the other four, Raphaela, Michaela, Gabrielle or Lucille? Staring at the screen will get her nowhere.

She opens the message. Urielle's icon of a Celtic redhead playing a harp is top centre. Underneath is, *Please complete this customer satisfaction survey about the services I provided six months ago. I would suggest you brew a pot of British Breakfast tea before settling down to complete this.*

What the devil? If it were any angel except Urielle she would put this down to spam and trash it. It could still be a nasty. What harm can come from making tea? The message vanishes.

Uh-oh. Urielle does not want her involvement traced. She must be bending her programming rules again. This is going to be very bad. Might as well do as she suggests.

Just as she places the hot teapot on the bar, the café's door bangs open. A slender man with dark colouring in a pale grey tracksuit and carrying a holdall rushes in from the glare of the streetlights. A second look, she realises it is Detective Sergeant Kungowa Onai in disguise, his skin paler than normal and face makeup giving him a longer nose and higher built-up cheekbones. But his unchanged eyes are the giveaway. Sweat stains his suit and runs down his face. He drops onto a high stool at the bar nearest to her, setting his bag on the floor.

She pours the tea into the mug waiting on the counter.

Atsuo momentarily stops wiping a table, shrugs her shoulders and continues her task.

Kungowa grabs the mug and gulps down the drink. "I needed that." He slams the empty mug on the bar.

Samanda pours a refill.

He glances round the room and nods at the mug. "Does this mean what I think it does?"

His real question is, 'has Urielle intervened?' He had found out about the angel's unconventional methods while investigating her murder case. Neither of them would give her secret away. "Yes, you could say it's heaven-sent."

"Oh hell." His questioning brown eyes lock onto hers as he drinks his tea more slowly.

She can say nothing more until they are alone. "Would you like something to eat? I recommend the cherry pie." As soon as the words escape her, she knows what would have been has changed; he has avoided going to an extremely dangerous place. This is why Urielle has intervened.

Horror flashes across his face. His hand shakes. He carefully places his mug down and stares his hand into stillness. "I think cherry pie would be nice. Make those two pieces please."

* * *

Atsuo waves goodbye as she exits. Kungowa waves back, thankful she is finally leaving him alone with Samanda. "Thought she'd never leave."

"She's a good worker," Samanda replies. "Before you ask, no, Urielle didn't tell me anything. She just got me to prepare the tea. Where were you going?"

"Home." Saying this aloud makes him nauseous. "That's the only place they'd be certain to catch me. I choose my route there based on the dice roll."

"Oh hell. You're welcome to use my spare bed."

The offer promises safety. "Thank you, but no. Can't risk putting you in the firing line."

She glances at her closed-down till. "I think I'm already there, don't you?"

Her calmness, enhanced by her cool blond hair and pale skin, irritates. "A single message like that would look like a coincidence. Let's keep it that way."

"If you say so." She pulls off her net to let her hair fall down and comes to the bar's front to face him. "What if Urielle decides you need more help?"

This simple question hides her real one. Urielle had found it easier to communicate with her than him. He has puzzled over why. Best guess is his detective's training gets in the way; the forever asking what alternative explanations could there be. "She'll find a way if she has to."

"If she can't?" She goes over to get her coat from the rail. "Best tell me what you're investigating in case she goes cryptic on me."

"Can't. Case confidentiality."

Her face turns bleak with a 'are we going to have to do this the hard way?' look.

He has gone undercover for a reason. It was the only way of finding out how the money laundering at Laceys fitness and beauty centre is being done. He is sure its owner, Leonid Abakumov must know about it as the money has been traced to his accounts, but proof is elusive. It is now also dangerous. They must have sussed he is an undercover detective. How did they do that?

His disguise as an orderly shunting patients and supplies around the hospital had been meticulously set up. He had made sure of that. Yet they and Urielle broke his cover. The angel he can understand. She has massive predictive capabilities that can find the out-of-pattern details and work them through. The same must be true for the criminals' capabilities.

"Oh my God," he whispers.

Those capabilities put the money launderers in a super league. His colleagues had grossly underestimated them. Explaining to his boss he knows his cover was broken because an angel had arranged to make him tea would be laughed out of court.

He finds Samanda staring intently at him. He stands. "All right, but at the first hint of any danger, you contact Renee, my boss. That understood?"

"That bad?"

How does she do that? Leapfrog to the next conclusion beyond the logical and obvious. "Scarily so." He picks up his holdall and heads for the door. "Does your offer of a bed tonight still stand?"

"Damn right it does."

"Come on, I'll tell you all about it on the way there," he says, stepping through the door and holding it open for her.

She sets the alarm and locks the door behind her. They head south past other lit shop windows.

"You know I've been doing workouts at Laceys gym, don't you?"

She stops to looks him up and down in an exaggerated manner. "Couldn't miss it."

It makes him laugh. "They've had loans propping them up, worth far more than their assets. It's a standard warning sign for money laundering. Our geeks tried to trail the money, but came to dead ends. The loans have recently increased significantly. So, they sent me in under a false profile, a hospital orderly who needed beefing up."

She sniggers. "You should try working at a café. Has the same effect without the need to pay gym membership fees."

* * *

Samanda's aching legs become too painful to ignore. It had been an extra-long day on her feet. Time to rub in some arnica, a remedy her grandmother had foisted upon her and surprisingly worked. Damn! It is in the bathroom cupboard and Kungowa is taking a late-night shower. She will have to wait.

She rubs the more painful calf muscle. Facing danger maybe part of his job, but even so. She switches to rubbing her other calf. Giving him shelter for a night helps. What more can she do?

The ache in her legs worsens. She wonders how much longer he will be in her bathroom and rubs her legs more vigorously. She stops mid-stroke and looks at them.

The recurring pain is a genuine reason to get advice, if not actual help from Laceys. What harm would it do if she visited them?

She rushes to her bedroom, packs her tracksuit and trainers in a bag and dumps it next to the front door.

"What's that for?" Kungowa asks from behind.

She turns round. He is in her spare bathrobe back to his normal dark skin colour and face shape, rubbing his tightly curled hair with a towel. The steely look in his brown eyes suggests he already knows the answer. "Going to Laceys before work tomorrow. Really need to do something about my aching legs."

"Absolutely not. It's too dangerous."

"Nice of you to be concerned. But as a free citizen, you can't stop me."

* * *

Kungowa hates the hippy disguise he bought at the shopping mall. The longhaired wig makes his head itch. As for acting the part of a laid-back has-been, it goes against his tenseness and makes him clumsy. On entering his police station, he reverts to character. He marches into his boss's office, rips off his wig and drops it onto her desk.

Detective Inspector Renee Stavinski sitting behind her desk goes white. "You're supposed to be dead."

The comment shocks. He drops down onto a chair. "Slight change of plan," is all he can come up with. He closes his eyes to take a moment to calm himself. "What happened?"

Colour is returning to her face. "Your block of flats suffered a massive gas explosion at three-thirty this morning. The fire service is still there putting out the fire."

He feels sick, but keeps it together. "Casualties?"

"That's the bizarre thing. We don't know. The auto-receptionist suffered a glitch and did not send backup data to central. No idea of who went in or out since early evening."

His eyes widen. Such a thing is almost unheard of with all the backups in place. This is a sophisticated intervention by the criminals. Or by Urielle? "Found any bodies yet?"

"No, but they haven't accessed all of the building yet."

He nods. This was an Urielle intervention. That will have taken some doing to get and keep all the other eighteen people out of the building.

"What?" Renee asks.

He looks her over. The angel will have predicted him visiting Renee, which means being told about his fake death is a good thing. He grabs his wig and puts it back on. "Looks like I'd better stay dead for now. Make sure you're the only one here who knows otherwise."

"Agreed. You're going straight into witness protection." Her hand reaches for her phone.

He snatches it away from her. "Absolutely not. I've got a job to finish." He dare not tell her about Samanda going to Laceys.

She rises to lean over her desk and despite her small frame towers over him. "I'm ordering you off the case."

He stands nose to nose with her. "This is far bigger than you or me."

"Which is why I want you out."

"You won't get another chance like this."

She narrows her eyes. "What're you not telling me?"

He stays silent.

"An inside job? One of us a traitor?" she finally asks.

That possibility shakes him. He had not thought of it. Why not? He had focussed on an angel-like predictive capability that would give the same results. He locks onto her green eyes. "I can't rule it out."

"Shit," she slumps into her chair. She rests her elbows on the table and her head in her hands before looking up. "Where do you think you slipped up?"

"Wish I knew. I'm going to disappear." The only hope of breaking this case now lies with Samanda, who should be nowhere near it, damn the stubborn woman.

* * *

Laceys screams understated plushness with its lack of advertised prices and streamlined lemon, spring green and grey foyer. The arced reception desk guards double doors either side. One is labelled, gyms, swimming pool and restaurant. The other leads to beauty salons, hairdressers and massage parlours. Samanda joins a short queue for the three receptionists. One nods a hello to a male athlete who swipes his phone over reader for the door leading to the gym. A woman leaves the desk and wobbles in her stiletto heels through to the beauty parlours. A grey-haired tight-muscled man exits after paying his annual subscription fee. Samanda reaches the desk and smiles.

"How may I help?" a young man with immaculately combed short black hair says.

"Can you do something to relieve my aching legs?"

"That would depend on the cause. May I ask if you have any idea what it is?"

Samanda wants to say yes to ruffle his customer-facing smoothness. "Working on my feet all day."

He glances her up and down. "We would recommend a full assessment package. It includes checking bone and muscle alignment, blood tests and life vitals."

"I just want to get rid of the aches now," she waves her hands emphasize her frustration.

"In that case, we would suggest a feet and legs spa and massage, though we cannot guarantee you will get complete satisfaction."

"How much?"

An I-thought-so smile flicks across his face. He does a few taps on his screen and a price shows up on the small screen facing her. It is expensive. But having revitalised legs will be heaven-sent. "Do you have someone free at the moment?"

"I'll check." He does a few more taps on his screen and waits for a response. His eyebrows rise slightly. "It would appear we've just received a cancellation. I've put that appointment on hold for you. Could you please place your hand on the desk pad," he nods to what looks like a stiff grey sponge pad on the desk in front of her, "until it turns green."

"Why?"

"It checks for basic health anomalies like high blood pressure, a requirement by law for any massages, no matter where."

"Oh." She does as asked. Is this how they recognised Kungowa as a police spy? She moves her hand away when it turns green.

"If you could please swipe in your ident and payment," he smirks.

This she does.

On reading his screen, the receptionist's face switches from smug to being surprised. "I see you're a completely new customer here. We've given you a twenty per cent discount on this visit."

She is sure their website said ten per cent earlier this morning. "Thank you."

"You're welcome. Please go to parlour twenty-two. Lit arrows will guide you there." He nods towards the door marked beauty salons. "Enjoy your visit." The smirk is back.

Samanda, glad to be away from him, finds her way to the room on the first floor. Its door opens as she approaches. Not only is this place plush, it is slick. A recliner chair is in the room's centre with armchairs and a coffee table to one side, a sink in the corner and bench on the other side with cupboards above and below. A female in functional green tunic and slacks is checking a screen on the bench. Her long brown hair is tightly tied back into chignon and her face glistens with well-oiled moisture.

"Welcome, Ms Cheney. I see this is your first time with us," the employee's teeth outshine her skin.

"It is, um, I didn't catch your name?"

"Alyssha, but many just call me Ali. May I ask if you had coffee or tea for breakfast?"

"Coffee. Why?"

"That would explain your elevated blood pressure."

"Is that a problem?"

"Goodness me, no." She takes out a bowl of wrapped sweets from an upper cupboard and offers it to her. "Have one or two of these? They contain citrus, spinach and herbal products to help lower your blood pressure, which in turn will give longer term benefits to your legs."

"I hadn't expected this."

Ali's smile lights up the room again. "We aim to give a holistic service."

"I see." She pops it into her mouth. Despite the hideous list of ingredients, its mixture blends to give a freshening zing, much like tender spring vegetables in lemon vinaigrette. "Interesting flavour."

"Please take a couple for later on."

"Thanks." Tucking them into her handbag she eyes the recliner. She is being treated far too well. "What comes next?"

* * *

Kungowa still in his disguise waits on a bench across the precinct from Laceys. He flicks through his messages on his cheap smartphone while keeping an eye on the entrance. His wig is distractingly itchy. There Samanda is, leaving and turning towards Romulisa.

The jauntiness in her walk is new, and something else that jars. It takes a few moments to pinpoint it. Her head does not bob up and down in coordination with her footsteps. He rubs his eyes to make sure he is seeing it correctly. Yes, he is.

He waits to see if anyone will follow her. Two people leave Laceys, but to his relief head in other directions. Once Samanda is out of view, he stands and saunters towards her café via a different route, making sure his worry does not make him walk too fast.

Romulisa is busy and he has to queue for his coffee. He pretends to read more messages, while sneaking glances around the place. Strangers seem ordinary, but experts know how to blend in. He keeps checking. The queue moves forward enough to glimpse the counter staff: Atsuo and a couple of other regular helpers, but no Samanda. Where is she?

There she is, behind the coffee-making machine. Good, except her head still does not line up with her movements. He reaches the counter.

"What can," she hesitates, "I get you?"

What part of his disguise is not working? "A large Americano and a breakfast wrap to have in please. Make that two Americanos. Need the caffeine."

She sets the coffee machine going. "That stuff raises your blood pressure, so they told me at the gym after they took my ident via their health-check pad." She places a breakfast wrap on a plate and adds the wrapped-up sweets from her pocket to his tray. "Try these. Supposed to be lemon, vegetables and herbs. Whatever, they've an interesting taste. It's what Laceys gave me to relax."

He had never been offered those. They must have known he was an undercover agent from the start, which would fit in with their predictive capabilities scenario. Her hint about them possibly being drugs could explain her strange lack of coordination. "Thanks. I'll try these later." He pockets them.

She places his steaming coffees from the machine on the tray and stares at his hands. "May I make a suggestion?"

"Sure," wondering what is coming next.

"Your outfit would be complete with some nail polish to match your clothes."

He looks down at his spread-out fingers. It is the one part of him not in disguise. That is how she recognised him. "Thanks for the tip," he smiles and takes his tray to a table outside.

* * *

The final remnants of the surreal perception vanish by the time Samanda reaches her flat that evening. What the hell was in those sweets? Choosing comfort food for supper, she digs out a ready-to-cook spaghetti and meatballs dish and thrusts it into her microwave. How many people do they give those damned things to anyway? It would certainly lessen the angels' workload.

She freezes. Urielle would have noticed the reduction in her workload and traced its cause. Surely that is a good thing, unless those sweets had long-term side effects?

If Urielle can identify the reduction, so would other similarly sophisticated prediction programmes. Some of them would have sent out automated alerts. It would imply…

Her microwave pings and its door unlocks with a click.

The results deliberately suppressed. That cannot be possible. Someone would have publicised this. She rushes into the lounge and grabs her smartphone to search for any news on this and stops. Whoever is locking down the media reports will pick up her search. Shudders frizzle down her back. She must be more careful.

She rubs her forehead as if she has a headache. A single automated web-wide app left will not catch every report. Items not quite fulfilling criteria rules would slip through. It needs real time reactive backup activities for a complete blockage, the kind of monitoring angels do…

Her phone pings an incoming message. It has a purple tag, shade 7851a9. She opens it. It is from Urielle.

I notice you have not completed the customer satisfaction survey I sent yesterday morning. Please do so now as I need the results for analysis.

Huh? Oh! This is the angel's way of getting her to report back. She opens the survey.

There is just one question. *Do you think the services angels provide are too intrusive?*

She hits ten on the scale, indicating they are far too meddling. As an afterthought she adds a comment, *Which one? Raph—*

Her smartphone wipes the first part of Raphaela's name. She tries to type it again. Same problem. She stares at the screen.

"Oh no," she says as the chain of logic drops into her mind. Raphaela's job is to ease people's stress and depression. Those sweets would do that. Has she found a way to break through the block of prescribing such drugs? Must have. The money laundering comes into the scheme somewhere. How? Of course, she needed to set up an innocent looking outlet to distribute those sweets and that needed money.

She drops to her seat. Hell, this is an angel war between Raphaela and Urielle. What can she do it about it?

Samanda glances at her screen. The survey has disappeared.

* * *

Kungowa hates the smell of overflowing alcohol at late night bars. Click-clacks of the pool tables out back can be heard over the tinkling glasses and hum of voices. The happy-to-contented atmosphere is reassuring, but not surprising. Shaughnessy does not tolerate rowdy behaviour, which is why he chose this place. He slouches over the bar where the CCTVs cannot see his face, sipping his whisky, waiting.

Renee sits down on the empty stool beside him, wearing workday green slacks and white blouse to compliment her oval face and brown hair. "Hello, stranger. Almost didn't recognise you."

He is not surprised: his hair dyed white, skin shaded darker with extensive pretend white tattoos on his arms and legs and added white bushy eyebrows. Sloppy grey T-shirt, jeans and sandals enhance his labourer aura. "Like it?" he slurs in a pretend southern accent.

"Not bad." She catches the bartender's eye.

He comes over. "Margarita please."

"And another one of these," Kungowa says waving his half-empty glass.

They watch and wait as the drinks come along. The bartender moves on to his next customer.

Renee takes a sip. "You're right about those sweets."

"What's the dope?"

"Sundownerlax. A new nasty hyper-addictive. Makes people relaxed so they go back for more. Trouble is it's easy to get too relaxed and stop the heart."

He fills in the rest. The sweets are low doses. Laceys' customers would ask for more and more, until they were given larger doses by an outside contact.

"I'm sending in two new undercovers tomorrow to take delivery of some sweets, though they won't know the mark until the last minute."

"Don't."

"Why not?"

"We don't know how they spotted me."

"That's why I'm bringing them in from outside."

He spreads his hands palm down on the bar. That pad must have been how they had caught him. Samanda had hinted as much. "It won't work."

"They're experts." She takes a sip and makes a play of enjoying its taste.

"Even so."

She gulps. "How?"

"Gyms are required to do medical checks before they allow anyone to do serious workouts. I reckon they've got the cyber accesses."

Horror grows on Renee's face. "Shit. They'll know we're onto them, won't they?"

"Yep."

She takes a few seconds to respond. "Leave this with me."

He nods; sure, she will use an informant who already has form instead. It is what he would do in her place.

* * *

Samanda is back at Laceys, unlucky to be facing the same smirk-face receptionist. "I'd like to talk to one of your managers please."

A hint of alarm flashes across his face. "Do you have a complaint about our service?"

"No. I've a deal proposal."

His mouth moves like a goldfish's to utter silent words. He finds his voice. "What kind of proposition?"

"That's mine and your managers' business. Is one available at the moment?" she nods towards his desk screen. "Chop, chop."

His fingers start typing.

A well-muscled man in an expensive streamlined business suit enters reception from the door to beauty salons. So clean-shaven his skin outshines his amber eyes and sleek dark brown hair. An auto-smile accompanies his outstretched hand. "Hello, Ms Cheney. I'm Leonid Abakumov, Laceys' owner."

She steps away from the desk and shakes his hand. "Good of you to come out here to meet me. How did you…?" she nods towards ex-smirk-face.

"Our AI monitors the building for issues."

"I see." Angels do spot-checks like that to catch occurrences of the very low probability events. A place like this with so many people coming through would be a good place to catch people behaving out of character. She wonders whether Raphaela thinks the probability of her investigation extremely low or minimal?

He waves his hand towards the door he came through. "Shall we go to my office?"

"Happy to."

He leads her along the deep-carpeted corridor to his office at the back. Its four armchairs facing each other across a conference table are in front of a large desk with a super-comfort swivel chair. The décor is the same as the rest of the place, minimalist in comforting colours. She takes an invited seat at the table.

"Any refreshment?" he asks.

"No thanks. I need to go into work when we're done here. Let's get down to business."

"A woman after my heart." He takes a seat opposite her.

"I run the Romulisa café a couple of blocks away. You may have visited it in passing?"

He briefly looks away. "I haven't had the pleasure, though I pass it on my way home. Wondered why you seemed so familiar."

She smiles. "Your masseuse gave me some interesting sweets yesterday. They certainly had the desired effect. I looked up your supplier, only to find you make them yourselves."

He winces slightly. "My grandmother's recipe, with all approved food standards ingredients."

"That explains it. Any chance of letting me sell them in my café? Obviously we'd have to do a trial period to see how they go down with the customers first."

"It would certainly give me another stream of income." He rubs his all too smooth chin. "I'll think about it, consult with my partners, get an AI assessment and all that sort of thing."

There it is again, AI, which aligns with Urielle's hint that Raphaela came up with this drug-sweet scheme. Proving it is another matter. "Of course. If your AI is up to it, maybe it could suggest improvements in our scheme."

"That's a thought." His smile is too eager.

* * *

Kungowa in a homeless outfit sits on the pavement down from Romulisa with a begging cap in front of him, wondering why Samanda is late. He is about to make tracks towards her flat when he spots her coming up the precinct. She has an all too satisfied smile.

He checks behind her. Quite a few people are heading her way or window-shopping. One glance is not enough to identify if anyone is on her tail. He keeps glancing her way, as she gets closer. A few potential followers turn into the shops or cafés, but there are still too many.

"Please help," he says as she passes him.

She glances down. Her eyes widen slightly. She crouches down. "Can I get you cup of tea?"

"Thank you," he says loudly. More quietly he continues, "Gives me chance to see if anyone's following you."

Her smile disappears. He is thankful she does not look round. "Sugar?"

"No thanks. Just milk."

"I'll be back." She heads into her café.

He watches for anyone stopping nearby. A middle-aged woman looks into a window displaying summer clothes. A young man stands to check his phone. An elderly woman sits on the bench down from him, facing the café. There, that thin man who has just turned back, checking an old-fashioned paper pocket map. That shows training in trailing. Damn!

Samanda returns with a mug in one hand and a sandwich in the other. His stomach rumbles in appreciation. She hunkers down. "Thought you might like tuna and cucumber."

He smiles a thank you and eagerly sips the tea, his favourite British Breakfast blend. "You've been followed by a thin man in beige slacks and a white shirt. Short curly brown hair, dark eyes, white skin. Blends into the background here easily enough," he whispers. "What've you been up to?"

"Suggested a business deal to Laceys to sell sweets at my café. They're drugs, aren't they?" she whispers back.

"Of the very addictive kind. Don't take any more." He bites greedily into a sandwich. "This is good," he says loudly.

"You need an angel to help you out."

"Any particular one?"

"Raphe."

He swallows careful not to choke. "Not Urielle?"

"True, she's a good one, but Raphe is more what you're looking for."

The implication explodes in his mind. Raphaela is the villain behind all this. He knows that underneath his skin makeup, he has paled with shock. "Really?"

She nods.

Fear squirms his stomach into knots. A predictive angel could be ahead of them each step of the investigation. Raphaela will watch anyone who takes sweets out Laceys, including Renee's informant. Samanda will already be on her watch list, checking her out. The man following her is a decoy, meant to waste the police's time, or worse. "Hell."

She smiles. "Rather apt."

Her calmness shakes him. "What're you up to?"

"Good question." She glances at her café, her sightline passing over the thin man. "You're not going to like it."

"I don't now." Why is he getting so protective of her? Must be the greater danger she is in. "But nothing I say will stop you, will it?"

"Not with Urielle having my back."

The angel must have contacted her. Time to put his trust in her as well, though he cannot help say, "Don't get too overconfident."

"I won't. I wouldn't come across as credible if I did."

She really has thought this through. "What am I going to hate?"

"We need to connect the drugs to Raphe. I act as bait to follow the trail back to her, with you as my go-between. After all, us working together would be considered extremely unlikely after you arrested me."

"Triple hell," effectively admitting she has a point. "What next?"

* * *

"Thank you for coming at such short notice," Abakumov says, waving his hand towards the tiny kitchen. "As you can see, we've a small establishment, too small to mass produce the sweets if your trial turns out to be a success."

Samanda takes in what looks like a home kitchen in an old warehouse, something her secretly recording smartphone hidden in her pocket will not capture. Everything has been put neatly away after a day's work. A cardboard box labelled 'Laceys Sweets' sits on the worktop ready for collection. The surfaces glisten smoothness without scratches or dents, all new furnishings. She is sure this had been specially set up for her visit. "Surely we can deal with that if and when we succeed?"

A quavering smile vanishes on his face. "Starting a bigger production line takes time, planning and investment. We need to examine our options now."

"Why not let word get out a bit more first? That will give us a better idea of the likely demand and we can plan on that. Even better, we'll be able to hook investors."

His smile trembles. "Investors will want payback. They'll take a chunk of our profits. It's better to go it alone."

"Who says?"

"Not who, what. We did an assessment."

"That was a quick turnaround. I only suggested it this morning."

He blushes. "Our AI turns out to be very helpful."

She bites her lips. "Not the one that checks for trouble at your gym?"

"As it so happens, yes."

She whistles: not about it being powerful, but that he has admitted it. "Sounds like you've got a multi-tasker there. I presume it's licensed. Where did you get it from?"

"Why do you want to know?"

"You don't seriously expect me to follow the business advice of an AI I know nothing about?"

He raises his eyebrows. "I see your point. What if I said a guardian angel had directed me?"

She tilts her head. "Are you talking about one of the angel AIs?"

"Let's just say I went through a rough patch at one time, as you did not so long ago. Yes, we do our homework on you, though in your case there was more than enough publicity."

The referral to her own murder case makes her inwardly squirm. It is a timely reminder she is under Raphaela's microscope. But she has what she needs. His admittance together with official records, which she is sure Urielle will have preserved from active deletion, is enough to convict the angel. "Sorry to hear about your own past troubles."

"Happens to us all if we live long enough." He pushes the cardboard box towards her, smiling. "This is your first delivery."

She grabs the box and tucks it under her arm. "Thank you. Let's see how this trial goes?"

"Of course." His smile has turned predator-like.

* * *

Kungowa watches Samanda leave the warehouse and shake hands with Abakumov. He turns right. But instead of turning right to head for her flat, she turns left to walk back the way she came. What the hell?

He fingers his burner phone inside his pocket, wondering if he should call Renee for help. There is no obvious danger to Samanda. The last thing he wants to do is to break cover without a result and there is still no proof of Raphaela's involvement. He hobbles along at a distance, following her past the old brick-built warehouses and into the shopping precinct. She must be returning to Romulisa. Why?

Out of the corner of his eye, he sees the thin man who previously trailed her. This time he is in a tracksuit, pretending to be an evening jogger. Someone or some-angel must have got this man to watch her. Abakumov, Urielle or Raphaela? He puts as much distance between himself and the man as he dares.

Very few people are wandering about by the time she enters Romulisa, leaving the door open. The thin man jogs past her café and stops to do stretching exercises nearby. Kungowa hides in the shadow of a shop's doorway opposite. A CCTV turns towards the café, and then another. This is just too much.

He hobbles over to and stops by the door. "Anyone here?" he shouts.

His burner phone buzzes. Of all the times his phone should ring. He accepts the incoming call.

"Who's this?" Renee's voice comes across the phone.

"Er…"

"Kungowa?"

Urielle must have connected them. "Yes, it is. Get some officers over to the Romulisa café in the High Street fast. Something's about to go down."

"What?"

He is unsure. "Someone's about to be killed."

"On it."

He throws the phone to the floor and steps inside. The thin man rushes past him, pushing him out of the way. Kungowa regains his balance and dashes after him. The man heads to the far end and around behind the bar, knife in hand.

Mugs, one after another, are hurled from below the other end, making the would-be killer duck and dodge.

Kungowa dives over the bar into the shower of crockery, grabs the man's arm and pulls him down onto the floor among the broken shards. He twists the criminal over and puts a knee onto his back. The man tries to push up with his free hand, which Kungowa yanks back. "Stay down."

The man grunts. "Who are you?"

"Detective Sergeant Kungowa Onai. I am arresting for attempted assault." He reads the man his rights to sound of approaching sirens.

By the time two uniformed police enter, he is wearing his police badge round his neck and pulling the man up. "Take him out of my sight. Charge is attempted assault." He watches the man being walked out of the café. It is only then he turns to face Samanda.

She with not a single scratch on her sits on the floor holding an empty mug. Her face is whiter than normal, obviously in shock.

"You all right?" he asks.

"I am. Are you?"

An automatic yes dies on his lips. It would be a lie. He glances at the cuts on his own hands. "Not really. Just thankful you're safe, for now. Damn it! You were almost killed."

"Calculated risk, plus the fact I put my trust in Urielle." She looks directly at him.

He wants to hug her and kill at the same time for what she has put him through. He does neither. "We've still not got the evidence."

"About that." She pulls out her smartphone from under the bar and offers it to him. "I think you'll find my recorded conversation with a certain person of interest here. The bits about the AI assistance are rather juicy. The extra necessary evidence you'll need will be in records on the 'net."

"Did he admit...?"

"Not directly. It'll be enough for a search warrant. Especially when you take into account this." She pulls a sealed cardboard box from a cupboard and turns its Laceys label towards him.

There must be the drug sweets in there. That alone would close Laceys down, but the real criminals would move on. Raphaela could easily start up a new organisation, if she has not already. He glances round. The street cameras cannot see Samanda, only the café's two interior burglar alarm cameras can. Something makes him check those again. Their monitoring lights are off. Urielle must have switched them off. Their conversation has not been monitored. His eyes widen at the pile of unbroken mugs beside Samanda on the floor: she had planned all this.

"It's not over," he finally says.

"What's not over?" Renee says coming through the entrance.

"The arrests, paperwork and further investigations." He pulls his current wig and throws it on the bar. "Hate these damned things."

"What arrests? You've got the perp."

"He's a minnow. Might even have been hired in especially for this job."

Samanda stands and pushes the box over towards Renee. "You'll find the contents of this interesting. I'm willing to swear under oath Leonid Abakumov, owner of Laceys gave them to me."

Renee looks from Samanda to the box to Kungowa. "You let an ordinary citizen get involved in this?"

"Had little choice. She out-stubborned me."

Renee turns back to Samanda. "Is this true?"

"Yes. I've got more evidence you need to see, but first I'm going to need police protection on my terms until you stop who's behind Abakumov."

"What about this café?" Kungowa asks.

"Atsuo can run it in my absence."

Renee purses her lips. "You'll get your police protection on one condition."

"What's that?"

"Kungowa also accepts police protection."

"That's blackmail," he says.

Renee drums her fingers on the bar, staring at him. The lights on the café's cameras are still out.

"Only on the same terms as Samanda's."

Renee's fingers stop drumming. "That is the most sensible thing I've heard from you in too long a while. Now, would someone mind telling me what's going on?"

*　*　*

Samanda wonders why after all the arrests and court cases she is being called in to visit Kungowa's boss. Once a police AI had examined her statement, it logically deduced Raphaela was behind the whole scam: Abakumov had made the mistake of admitting his connection to Raphaela. She had been switched off and her executable code deleted, much to Samanda's relief. It meant she could get some way back to an ordinary life running Romulisa.

She is shown into Renee's office. Kungowa is there, sitting in one of the chairs opposite his boss.

Renee stands, smiles and shakes her hand. "Please sit."

Samanda relaxes and sits. Whatever this meeting is about, it is has all the signs of being friendly. "What can I do for you?"

"First let me congratulate you on your impending bravery award."

This is news to her. "Me?"

"Yes, you."

"What about Kungowa? Without him..."

"I disobeyed direct orders," Kungowa says.

"Oh."

"And it's part of my job," he adds.

"The commissioner is awarding you a commendation anyway." Renee does not look happy about it.

Kungowa's eyes widen in clear surprise.

"Congratulations," Samanda says.

"Um... thank you."

"I just have two questions," Renee says.

"Only two?"

Renee's smile seems too angelic. "For now." She turns to Samanda. "How did you switch off your café's burglar alarms? We lost valuable time because of that."

She shrugs her shoulders. "I didn't. Raphaela might have had something to do with it." It is not a lie, only speculation. At least, that us what she tells herself. She is sure Urielle had been pushed into switching them off to let her and Kungowa could talk freely before Renee arrived. It covered her own mistake of mentioning the angel by name, which the angel must have predicted would happen.

"Just checking. We think that's the most likely explanation, though we'll never be certain."

"What's the other question?"

"You and Kungowa seem to make a good team. I was wondering if you'd consider joining the police, either full time or as an on-call civil police?"

Samanda's jaw drops. What the hell has Urielle done? Sounds like the angle thinks they will have more cases to solve in the future.

Rosie Oliver's debut novel is available through Amazon.

A Way Out
Sarina Bosc

"If they find out you smuggled that thing in, they'll put you in the Suspension Chamber for a week."

"I didn't smuggle it in. We have a symbiotic relationship." The words come out short as I try to focus on what my beard is doing. At least, it looks like a beard to everyone else. "Hurry it up, will you?" Chin tucked, I mumble the request at the wiry-haired creature slowly burrowing into the lock.

"Well, whatever you want to call it, *you* got arrested—not it."

My cell mate, Coz'el, isn't wrong. The last thing I want is to be deprived of every single sense in a Chamber. But his personal opinion is coloring this conversation. I'm sure if I was a smuggler, trafficker, or politician, Coz'el would be fine with me trying to find a way out.

The 'it' Coz'el refers to is Chirp. I don't know what Chirp is in terms of species or where he's from. We came across one another decades ago, and he's been with me ever since. He's gotten me out of a few tight spots and I'm hoping this is another we can add to the list.

As Coz'el and I banter, Chirp reaches salt-and-pepper tendrils carefully into the lock. It's a delicate job, one he hasn't had to do before, because this is my first time in Xidcore, the largest prison in the galaxy.

Coz'el is no stranger to the institution that free-floats a few thousand units away from any other planet or colony. My nose wrinkles at the scent of the iron door as he begins to tell me about a smuggling deal that went wrong just south of Tingrin, a planet I'm only vaguely familiar with. Chirp crinkles in annoyance, then does a little wavering stretch forward. With a sigh, I press my cheek against the pitted surface to help him out.

Coz'el likes to chat. A lot, for a guy who claims to hate me with every ounce of his being.

"What's your plan after this?" he asks, slit pupils narrowing in curiosity. "There's nowhere to go once you're out of here." Then he launches into a story about how, the third time he got out, he managed to catch a ride on a stray asteroid. Two fingers on his left hand were blast-frozen off during the ordeal.

"Don't worry about it," I grit out. Chirp's movements tug at the sensitive skin of my upper lip and I wince.

Xidcore is unlike other prison systems in that there is no uniform. Myself and every other inmate here are completely naked. It's a jarring lesson in the anatomy of intergalactic species, and it leaves my tattoo exposed—the raised one on my chest that looks infected, but isn't.

The whole reason I'm in here is going to be how I escape. But I'm not about to tell Coz'el that. Oddly, the devices I make don't work around certain substances. Iron is one of them; the mineral Derophun another, as well as a particular flower found on a nameless planet in the seventy-fifth quartex. If a TimeVault comes into contact with any of the above, it'll shut down immediately. Or implode.

Honestly, it's anyone's guess which one it'll be.

If Chirp gets us out and I can make it to the canteen, the aluminum housing that makes up the rest of the prison shouldn't have an effect on the device. I'll be able to get out of here just long enough to put together a plan for when I materialize back here a day later.

The massive lock clicks. Coz'el and I freeze. Chirp goes comically stiff.

We listen to the sound of iron balls shifting, pins clicking, an intricate and impressive chorus.

"You don't think you deserve your sentence?" Coz'el asks now that it's dawning on him that I might actually get out.

I give him a sour glance. We've been in this cell for three months, long enough for the Rastu guards to write me off as a non-threat. No one quite knows what I am, but being compliant and agreeable gets you ignored quickly.

"Selling your product to Humans is cruel, isn't it? With how ravaged their planet is now. I heard one of the supers saying you were probably the reason for thousands of Wharf jumps—"

Guilt sweeps through me. Wharf jumps aren't a great way to go. Throwing yourself out into space like that, blast-freezing every cell in your body. It's quick, hopefully—I wouldn't know.

"I didn't make them do it," I mutter, annoyed to be tied to potentially thousands of suicides. It's not like I discovered, or encouraged, Wharf jumps.

The thing is, the super might be right. But so what? I did it out of sympathy; that's what I told the High Court, but they were too focused on money as motive. If they looked at the numbers, they'd see I was basically evening out as far as income and spending. What it costs me to make a TimeVault is nothing compared to what Humans get in return. A chance to see their planet before it was destroyed; to see loved ones again or, if they're morbid, to go back to the few moments that doomed them.

On every planet in every galaxy, those moments always seem miniscule and unimportant. But as the Humans learned—the last few thousand of them, anyway—those moments add up.

They're a dying species. I was driven by compassion. Why else would I choose to sell TimeVaults in that choking wasteland? If some returned, realized that going back couldn't change anything, and decided to take an easy way out—was that really the wrong choice?

But the High Court convicts based on the morals and ethics of the victim species, so here I am. If Humans hadn't vetoed the option of assisted suicide in their past, maybe they'd have another way out. For the remainder of the species, all that's left is a stifling death as their oxygen and water supplies dwindle.

Chirp shivers and I twine my fingers in the rough hair, calming him. "Well, it was good knowing you."

Coz'el still looks unconvinced. The door opens with only a brief squeak. I slip out of the cell and make a run for it.

Down this block, then a stairwell. Through two doorways; the Rastu guards here are both molting, so they're slow to respond when I appear. Their bodies under the hard carapaces, half-hanging from their torsos, are soft and sluggish. I lose them easily with two left turns.

Then I'm standing in the canteen with the huge arched ceiling overhead. My fingernails dig into the raised tattoo; a small capsule slips out. A TimeVault I buried in my own skin about eight years ago.

I never wanted this. There's nothing for me to go back to—it's been so long that no one even knows what species I am, where I belong. Unlike Humans, I won't have a planet to get nostalgic about or a specific event that ties me to *home*.

But this is my only way out. I'll take the TimeVault, have a day to consider my options, and then reappear. Right here, in Xidcore's canteen, hopefully with a plan.

So I swallow the capsule dry and think of what I want to see: the meadows Humans have mournfully described when they come back from a Vault. A day full of warm rain and moisture-heavy air. Clouds, fragrant dirt, delicate flowers hidden in the grass.

All things too good to be true. A promise; something to return to.

Something that we no longer have.

Everything goes white.

Sisters
Toni Artuso

Rupert Ware, CEO of Dreams Embodied Vacations, Ltd., confronted Jerzy Petosky across a conference table that felt to Jerzy as wide as a football field. In addition to a mahogany gridiron, a curtain of e-cig vapor also separated them as Ware puffed furiously. "It took you and your associate long enough to get here," he groused as Jerzy and Mike took seats across the table from him. Kevin Silva, DEV's head of security, who'd shown them in, slunk around the corner to sit on his boss's left but at a discrete distance. *Maybe he's afraid of Ware's bite*, Jerzy mused, suppressing a smirk. "I do hope you realize time is of the essence here?" Ware continued blustering.

"Yes, sir, we understand that," Jerzy nodded, hoping to sound chastened but failed to stop himself from adding, far too casually, "but, of course, your call surprised us since you assured me that, with your foolproof, state-of-the-art security system, I'd never hear from you."

"I've got a rentee in extreme distress here, Detective," Ware snapped. "She's experiencing increasing gender-dysphoric trauma even as we speak. If she goes to the media, DEV will be ruined—ruined!" he repeated, slamming his fist on the table. "Now, Silva here," he waved his left hand dismissively in his direction, "claims you're the best in the business. It's time for you to live up to that reputation!"

Jerzy leaned forward, folded his hands, and put his elbows on the table. "Kevin here," he nodded to Silva, "assures me that the scanning equipment at your exit did not malfunction nor was there operator error. And, now that you've verified the body in question walked out of your facility without setting off any alarms, no sensor sweeps can find any trace of the body's subdermal microchip."

Silva coughed into his right fist and grunted. "We're already gone over this, Jerzy."

Jerzy held up his hand and continued, "And you've put out an APB with law enforcement and heard nothing."

"That's right," Ware took another drag on his e-cig.

Mike, Jerzy's junior partner, leaned forward in his chair and cleared this throat, ignoring Jerzy's warning frown to be quiet. "Any idea how this happened?"

"How the hell should I know?" Ware nearly screamed. "That's what I pay you smartasses—I mean, people—to figure out!"

Jerzy cleared his throat. "We'd like to interview the distressed rentee." *Let her be less hysterical than this guy*, he prayed.

* * *

When Kevin tapped on the door of the resort's luxury penthouse suite, a male voice answered from within, "Come in."

"She doesn't sound too upset," Mike muttered.

Kevin shrugged. "That's her husband talking." With that, he opened the door. Inside, they found a pair of men, one standing, rubbing the back of the other, who sat at a glass table positioned at a window overlooking the DC skyline. The seated man slumped in a pink, floral dress, head in hands.

"Mr. and Mrs. Greene," Kevin said, "This is Jerzy Petoskey and Mike Mindoch—the consulting detectives we told you about."

The standing fellow reached out and introduced himself as he shook Jerzy's and Mike's hands. "I'm Harry Greene. I understand you folks are the best in the business."

Before Jerzy opened his mouth, Mike blurted, "That's right." Jerzy scowled at Mike, but his junior partner ignored his silent reproof.

"And this is my wife, Silvia," Harry reached down and rubbed the shoulders of the seated man. "Why don't you say, 'Hi,' dear?" he prodded gently, as if coaxing a toddler recovering from a temper tantrum.

Sniffling heavily, Silvia looked up. Jerzy didn't think it possible, but Silvia Ramirez Greene looked more distraught than Ware. Waterproof mascara that clearly failed to stand up to tears streaked the seated man's cheeks. "You two gonna find the thief who's got my body?" she demanded in a nasally voice.

Jerzy, his hand on Mike's right shoulder, squeezed hard to shut him up. "We'll do our best, ma'am," he replied levelly, deadpan. Briefly, he glanced over his right shoulder and fixed Mike with a gaze that, he hoped, said, *That's how it's done. A pro neither brags nor overpromises.*

"Your best?" Silvia bawled. "What the fuck!" The man burst into tears and buried his face in his wiry arms.

Harry offered the two detectives an apologetic smile and resumed rubbing his wife's shoulders. "They're here to help ..." he soothed.

Silvia raised his head and blew his nose loudly. "At least he called me 'ma'am,'" he muttered and turned a tear-streaked face toward Jerzy. "You've *no* idea what this is like—to be trapped in a body of the wrong gender!"

For once, Jerzy didn't need to jump in ahead of Mike. The younger man shrank back from the volatile Silvia. "No, ma'am," Jerzy agreed. "I can't know your suffering."

Silvia swallowed hard and muttered at his bare, shaved legs through the glass table, "I should never have agreed to a cross-gender body swap."

Harry squatted down beside his wife. "Honey, don't blame yourself. Remember how much better the money was than for the usual same-sex deal?"

Silvia whirled on him. "Shut up, Harry! Don't you want your wife back?"

Now that the victim turned her wraith toward someone else, Mike, emboldened, spoke up, "Ma'am, do you have any idea why he'd steal your body?"

"Isn't it obvious?" She threw out his hands. Jerzy noted how the red nail polish failed to hide the chewed edges. "It's some transperson, desperate to be a woman finally!"

Once more silenced by Silvia's outburst, Mike slunk back.

Embarrassed, Harry looked up at the two detectives. "I'm sorry, gentleman," he apologized. "She's not herself. It's the testosterone making her aggressive. You remember from puberty," he shrugged. "It takes a while to control it."

Silvia said nothing but only stared daggers at Harry through tears.

Jerzy nodded. "Mrs. Greene," he leaned over and patted a hairy wrist. "We'll get you your body back as quickly as possible."

* * *

As Jerzy and Mike plummeted downward in the elevator, ears popping, Kevin cleared his throat. "I think this is the work of our competitor."

"TCTF?" Jerzy asked, skeptical.

Mike scowled, "Who?"

"Trans Corpus Trans Formations," Kevin gushed, warming to his theory, "they also offer body-swapping vacation packages, and they'd *love* to smear us by claiming our security's lax."

"Interesting theory," Jerzy offered noncommittally as they stepped off the elevator into DEV's gleaming front lobby. He turned and offered his hand to his client. "We'll keep in touch, Kevin; meanwhile, chin up, and, of course, let us know the minute you hear anything."

As the two private investigators stepped away, Mike offered, "I can check out that competing resort, like the client wants."

Jerzy replied only after they'd stepped out into the stifling August heat. "Don't waste your time," he shook his head. "If word gets out that a rentee's body vanished without a trace that won't dry up just *this* resort's supply of rentees," he gestured at the sparkling glass tower behind them, "it'll ruin the whole industry. Instead, run the renter's picture against facial recognition databases to find his real identity."

Ignoring this suggestion, Mike lowered his voice and asked, in a conspiratorial tone, "What if it's an inside job? You know, Kevin's in on it?"

Jerzy shoved his hands in his pockets and sauntered toward the parking garage. "I've known Kevin a long time, so I doubt it, but, at this point, everyone's a suspect. If you've got the time, you know the drill: check Mr. Silva's financials to see if he may have suddenly been able to afford something he couldn't afford earlier."

Undeterred, Mike pressed Jerzy, "What about the victim's theory that it's a transwoman running off with her body?"

Jerzy came to an abrupt halt and, exasperated, threw his hands in the air. "Transphobic nonsense! There are plenty of good, old-fashioned, tried-and-true medical procedures for gender affirmation. Besides, any number of transmen and transwomen have paired up for completely voluntary, totally consensual body swaps. No, something else is going on."

As Jerzy resumed his walk to the garage, Mike continued in his wake, prodding, "All right, so while I'm running endless database searches to try and ID our body snatcher, what will you be doing?"

Jerzy whirled on Mike, thinking, *You work for me, buddy, not the other way 'round,* but he only said, "I've got a contact who might shed light on this."

* * *

When Special Agent Timothy Flynn, his girth broader and his hair thinner than the last time they met, stepped into the conference room with its frosted glass windows, Jerzy stood and offered his hand.

Shaking it, Tim asked, hopefully, "Changed your mind about rejoining us?"

Jerzy shook his head as, like Tim, he sagged back into one of the cushioned chairs. "Not unless I get my old job back."

Tim scoffed. "No can do, buddy. It's verboten—international treaty ban and all that. Besides, do you *really* miss it?"

"I'm not the one missing it," Jerzy prodded, hoping to get a rise out of Flynn, but either his old contact missed the news, or he'd improved his poker face over the years.

"What are you talking about?" Flynn scowled.

Jerzy sighed. "There's a runaway body swapper on the loose—in a borrowed body."

Flynn's scowled deepened. "Don't the scanners prevent that? Rented bodies have subcutaneous chips that show up on sensor sweeps, right?"

Now, his old contact clearly played dumb. "We both know this agency has ways to hide those signatures."

"You know as well as I do that I can't discuss our operations," Flynn leaned forward and tapped his finger on the mahogany table, "but we're out of the body-swapping business for good." He waved a hand above his head to indicate the rarified air of the executive floors above. "That comes straight from the top. Believe me, you'd be the first to know if we got back into it."

Jerzy leaned forward, folding his hands and resting his elbows on the table. "Then I'm not the only former body-swapper who's missing their old job."

Tim grunted. "So whadda you want from me, Jerzy?"

"The name or names of whoever has the level of expertise to pull off a disappearance like this."

"I can't give you that information," Tim snorted. "I'm not cross-contaminating cells, even if those cells are inactive."

"It's too late for that." Jerzy slid a picture across the table at the special agent. "I've got the guy's face."

Tim picked up the photo. He said nothing, but his deepening scowl spoke volumes.

"Look, I just need a name," Jerzy tried to sound reasonable. "If I bounce this off enough photo databases, I'll get it anyway."

Flynn looked up as he dropped the photo back onto the desk. "If he's one of ours—and I'm not saying he is—you'll never find his real ID in any facial recognition database accessible to you."

Even though Tim called that bluff, Jerzy played another card. "You tell me who this is, and no one will ever know where or how I got this information."

"Or what?" Jerzy's contact crossed his arms over his chest.

"Or the news might leak—anonymously—that this supposedly foolproof body-swapping business—which *I've* never approved of for recreational use—is not foolproof, and that the government never should have licensed the tech to the private sector."

Tim's nostrils flared as he sighed, but the bureaucrat refused to admit defeat. "Look, Jerzy, I'll run it up the proverbial flagpole and get back to you."

* * *

At this hour, mid-morning, the drive from Langley to the hangars and warehouses huddled on the eastern outskirts of Dulles took a mere 30 minutes. Even though Jerzy's GPS cluelessly searched for the peeling Quonset hut that housed "Nationwide Trans Logistics Ltd.," his memory still served. Now overshadowed by a brand-new storage facility, the unprepossessing building's door swung inward with a creak so loud it almost drowned out the old-fashioned bell that jingled, signaling the entry of a potential customer.

"Coming!" a gruff male voice echoed from the back. "And shut the door! Don't let the cool air out ..."

Jerzy grunted as he considered the single oscillating fan by the cash register that attempted, valiantly but vainly, to move the place's stagnant air.

"Well, I'll be damned ..." A portly fellow with a mop of salt-and-pepper curls and a matching beard stepped up to the private investigator.

"Been awhile, Larry," Jerzy offered his hand.

Larry Stewart made a pretense of straightening his hopelessly crooked tie then shook Jerzy's hand. "So," he beamed, "you here to make the switch permanent? I've got a couple of interested transmen lookin' to hookup."

"No," Jerzy shook his head. "I'm here on behalf of the client—actually, the client's client. The woman's stuck in a man's body, and she's very dysphoric."

Larry waved at a desk covered with piles of paper and dusty computer equipment. "Sit down!" Larry indicated a cracked leather chair in front of the scuffed desk then sagged down in a chair behind it. Its squeak rivelled the door's. "Send her to me. I'll arrange something. Like I said, I've always got a transman or two on the line lookin' for a good permanent swap to a fit, youngish, healthy male body."

Jetzy sat tentatively in the guest chair. Despite its strident protests, it held his weight. "No dice. She wants her original back."

"Can't help her," Larry shrugged. "Not sure how I can help you, either."

Jerzy leaned forward and handed his old contact a picture of the rentee in his birth body, the one that Silvia Greene now inhabited with such intense distaste and ill grace. "Did this fellow try to arrange a swap?"

"Can't say for sure," Larry grunted and handed the picture back. "I gotta respect my clients' privacy, ya see?"

Sighing, Jerzy leaned forward, pulled out his wallet, and set a handful of bills on the desk in front of Larry. "Does this help your memory?"

The body broker snagged the bills, which he carefully counted then pocketed. "Yeah, I remember this fellow; came in, made some inquiries." Larry sighed, like a fisherman reminiscing about the one that got away. "He refused to make it permanent, so his potential match backed out."

"Yeah, but as a broker, you're not about to let a client—even a short-term one—walk. You must have a name—and contact info."

Larry shrugged again. "All I've got's a first name, and we both know it's fake: John, as in 'John Doe.' And, as for contact info, I've got a phone, but I'm sure it's the number of a burner phone and has been disconnected by now. After all, if your body bandit is in some woman's body, he's not waitin' on my call."

"All the same," Jerzy insisted. "I'd like the number."

* * *

Jerzy'd barely stepped out of Larry's so-called "office" into the eye-stinging late-morning sun when his cell phone came to life.

"It's Tim," the CIA special agent muttered on the other end of the line. "I, uh, spoke to the powers that be. They'll make an exception ..."

Tim's pause warned Jerzy to be ready for a catch. "That's great, but ..." he prompted.

"There's concern that the former agent in question poses a defection risk," Tim cleared his throat, "and, with it, potential intelligence compromise ..."

"You think whoever this is will sell the stealth tech that's allowing them to evade the scanners?" Jerzy hesitated a fraction of a second. With all major intelligence agencies out of body-swapping for good—thanks to the international treaties banning the technology—such stealth technology lacked value; however, if this bogus concern spooked the CIA higherups into releasing the info he needed, he must play along. "Who's in the market?"

"The Russians," Tim rasped, as if the very mention of their once-and-future opponents irritated his throat.

Jerzy placed his palm on his car's biometric scanner. Obediently, the vehicle's gullwing door silently slid up. *Of course*, he nodded to himself, *the eternal bogeymen*. "So you need me to head 'em off at the pass, before they give the goods to Ivan?"

"Actually, we'd like you to assess whether the Russians already have the goods in hand."

Jerzy scowled as he sank into the driver's seat. "What makes you think they'll talk to me?"

Tim cleared his throat discreetly. "It's, uh, my understanding that, thanks to earlier assignments, you uh, enjoy a special relationship with your Russian counterparts." He phrased that last part so delicately that Jerzy fancied he actually heard Tim's blush.

Jerzy grunted as the gullwing slid down. "Fair enough." He pressed the ignition to get the air conditioning blasting. "Send me the rogue retired agent's aliases first, though. Otherwise, I'm shooting in the dark."

"Will do," Tim agreed, "but you've gotta get back to us ASAP with what you learn."

"Deal," Jerzy agreed.

Bathed in blessedly cool, he rang off then barked at the car, "Dial office."

Before Jerzy said a word, Mike groaned and launched into a string of complaints. "I'm hitting nothin' but dead-ends. Your buddy, DEV's head of security, Silva, checks out—no fishy financials," Mike sighed, disappointed.

Jerzy squeezed his eyes shut, thinking, *I told you so ...*

Mindoch bulled onto his next point. "I'm afraid TCTF, DEV's competitor, checks out, too. They see this as an industrywide threat. No way they'd have a hand in this ..."

"Mike, why'd you ..." Jerzy started, but before he demanded why, with a hot case like his, Mike wasted time on red herrings, his junior partner interrupted him, "Got anything on the transgender angle?"

Jerzy swallowed hard, pushing down his growing irritation with his wayward partner. "My old contact in the body broker business recognized the suspect's photo, but his deal fell through when he refused to consider a long-term swap with a transman ..."

Mike interrupted. "Did you get a name, contact info, anything?"

Jerzy rubbed his furrowed forehead. What made Mike think he ran this operation? "Of course," Jerzy snapped, his irritation finally breaking through. "I'll share that all with you in a minute, though both the broker and I doubt that name and phone number are worth much."

"That's better than the goose egg I've got out of the facial recognition database search," Mike growled bitterly, as if he resented doing the one legitimate piece of work Jerzy asked of him.

"Then my last phone call just made your day. I'm about to send over a series of aliases to you that you can bounce off all those databases. Call me if you get any hits," Jerzy ordered.

"And what are you going to be doing?" Mike demanded, unphased by his boss's peremptory tone.

"I'm seein' a man about a horse," Jerzy muttered as he put his car into reverse and started backing out of NTLL's gravel parking lot.

* * *

"This is your idea of a hot lunch date?" Andrei Nemerov gestured contemptuously at a hot dog stand in the shadow of one of the skyscrapers that flanked DuPont Circle. "You know, back in the day, when I was buying, I took you nice places."

"That was then," Jerzy shrugged. "Besides, you're one of us now, an American. There's nothing more American than a good, ole dog."

"There are days when I regret not going over to the French," Andrei shrugged. "Their food's better."

"But you'd never have tracked down Lois," Jerzy smirked.

The hotdog vendor didn't appreciate Andrei and Jerzy's banter. "What can I getcha?" he barked.

"An American dog," Andrei replied, unnecessarily exaggerating his Russian accent. "With 'da works.'"

"Make it two, Andrei," Jerzy chided. "Remember, I'm buying."

"Big spender here say make that a double," Andrei chortled.

"I heard," the man shoved one hotdog at the big Russian while grabbing a second with his tongs.

As the pair settled onto a park bench, Andrei continued his good-natured interrogation. "To what do I owe the unexpected pleasure of your company? Clearly, you're no longer in a position to seduce me, and you don't work for the CIA anymore, so you can't be recruiting for them."

"We got a body bandit on the loose," Jerzy replied as he took a bite of his dog.

Andrei shrugged. "Sounds like a problem for the police, not your former employers. After all, no one body swaps for espionage anymore."

Jerzy cocked a skeptical eyebrow at Andrei, who sat to his left. "This body bandit's evaded all the sensors, left no trace. *That* requires industrial-strength spy-tech."

"Maybe CIA ought to keep better track of their toys." Andrei polished off his first dog.

"Maybe the body bandit figures they can cut a better deal when they defect if they throw some nice hardware into the bargain."

"You think the KGB would want a device that our mutual body-swapping ban has made obsolete?" Andrei countered as he sunk his teeth into the second dog.

Jerzy nodded. He didn't expect Andrei to buy Tim's crazy theory. Not even he, Jerzy, did. "None of your old contacts is crowing about getting a former CIA body swapper to defect?"

Andrei snorted. "Believe me, I'd be the first to rub your nose in it." He waggled a finger at Jerzy. "You tried to turn me."

Jerzy sighed, "See how well that worked ... Now you have cushy job at a beltway bandit. What is it? Future Threat Assessment Institute?"

"That is not work," Andrei flapped a dismissive hand. "Making PowerPoints all day—waste of time. Now," Andrei leaned forward and poked Jerzy in the chest with a pudgy finger, "assuming other identities and bodies and using those ... now *that's* real work!"

Jerzy nodded. He, too, missed the good old days, but he considered reminiscing pointless. "If you hear anything," he flipped an old-fashioned business card at Andrei, "you know where to find me." He stood. "Give my regards to the Missus. How's she doing?"

Andrei stood with a groan. "Oh, Lois? Fine, but she's gained some weight. I wish she took as good care of her body as you did when you were in it."

Jerzy smirked as he looked over the man he'd tried to seduce while inhabiting Lois Hanlon's body. He'd failed, of course, but, when the treaty ban ended all body swapping, Andrei did leave the KGB to hunt down the body Jerzy used. *That's what you get when you marry someone for their looks alone*, he thought, but he only said, "You know me: I always leave it better than I found it."

* * *

Jerzy just stepped into the elevator of the garage where he parked when his cell phone went off again. He grunted with satisfaction when he saw the call came from his office. Maybe Mike finally did something useful, despite himself.

"Did you see your man about his horse?" Mike demanded before Jerzy said a word.

Jerzy sighed. He'd hired Mike from the DC Metro Detective Division to work for him, not the reverse. "Yes, and as I suspected, my contact sent me on a wild goose chase, but I hope the information he gave me helped *you* find something."

"I cashed in some chips from back in the day, but I found a raft of court records for Kent Teagle ..."

Jerzy recognized that as one of the names Tim provided, apparently the former body-swapping agent's legal name, buried among the aliases. He interrupted Mike. "I hope you didn't waste a lot of political capital getting access to court records when they're publicly available ..."

Mike ignored him and bulled ahead. "The guy's in a custody battle with his ex over their kids: the eldest, Brian, is 12. His younger brother, Gabriel, is 10. There's a restraining order against Mr. Teagle ..."

Jerzy stepped out of the elevator onto his level. "That's not unusual," he grunted. "What's the ex alleging, spousal abuse?"

"No, the restraining order is for their kids. The ex says they don't want to see their father because they feel unsafe with him."

"Ouch," Jerzy winced as he made his way to his car. "He's a child abuser?"

"There are two sides," Jerzy heard Mike's shrug over the phone. "Mr. Teagle insists that this is a case of parental alienation. In fact, he claims that Mrs. Teagle, uh," the former DC detective paused to look up her name, "Gretchen Teagle—wait, make that *Dr.* Gretchen Teagle—is a narcissist, who has planted all these crazy stories in the kid's heads."

Jerzy tsked as he switched the phone to his left hand and ear to free his right palm to release his car's biometric lock. "What kind of Doctor is she? Professor? GP? What?"

"A shrink."

"Ole Kent's got his hands full trying to convince a judge that a shrink's crazy," Jerzy observed as he ducked under his vehicle's gullwing to slide into the driver's seat. "We got a lot of family drama here, but that's the judge's problem to sort. What's *our* bottom line?" He tamped down his irritation and decided, after this case, to talk to his junior partner about staying out of irrelevant ratholes.

"I'm worried this guy is planning to use the disguise of Mrs. Greene's body to do a noncustodial parental kidnapping and abscond to another country with the kids."

Silently, Jerzy conceded the plausibility of that threat. "Send over the doc's address. I hope she can see me between patients this afternoon."

"You're in luck. The doctor's not seeing patients today. Her office says she's at home, so I'll send you that address."

"Thanks, Mike," Jerzy rang off as he started his car spiraling down out of the garage.

* * *

When a Georgetown address popped into his GPS, Jerzy arched an eyebrow. Dr. Teagle possessed means to afford a tony neighborhood like that. He counted her proximity a stroke of luck since, even with mid-day traffic, it took only 20 minutes to reach her brownstone.

A well-kept middle-aged woman answered the door. "Can I help you?" she scowled.

"Sorry to disturb you, ma'am. My name's Jerzy Petoskey. I'm a colleague of your ex's from the Agency." Jerzy counted on the good doctor's willingness to talk to a government agent rather than a private investigator, so he withheld the fact he'd left the CIA.

A muscle on the right side of the woman's jaw twitched. "He's not here," she snapped. "Kent's left the Agency—and us, for good."

She went to close the door in Jerzy's face, but he kept it open, with a hand and a foot. "I've left the Agency, too, ma'am. Now I'm a private investigator. My client's Dreams Enabled Vacations, Limited."

"They've nothing to do with me or my family. We've done with body swappers." She pushed again, in vain. "Step back so I can close my door," she ordered.

"The reason I'm here, ma'am," Jerzy grunted as Dr. Teagle put her weight into pushing the door closed, "is that your ex has absconded with a woman's body. He could use her identity to engage in noncustodial parental kidnapping."

The pressure on Jerzy's hand and foot eased. The psychiatrist peered around the edge of the door. "You think Kent, in the guise of some strange woman, is planning to abduct my children?"

"Yes, ma'am," Jerzy panted. Having delivered his warning, he stepped back from the door, leaving her free to slam it in his face.

She sputtered, "That's absurd." She sounded unconvinced.

Jerzy pressed on this chink in her armor that this tiny sliver of uncertainty opened. "Do you know where your children are right now, ma'am?"

"Of course," she glared at him. "Brian's upstairs in his room." Dr. Teagle stepped back and, turning to the stairs behind her, called, "Brian, sweetie, come here!"

"Why?" a muffled but clearly truculent male voice, cracking with puberty, demanded from upstairs.

"I need to ask you something," she huffed, as Jerzy silently took satisfaction in surmising which parent supplied Brian's stubbornness.

"Okay," the voice huffed back. A gawky barefoot preteen in a t-shirt and shorts tumbled downstairs. At the bottom, he squinted up at his mother. "Whadda you want?" Then he spied Jerzy standing in the blazing afternoon sun outside. "Who's he?"

Dr. Teagle reached down and ran her fingers through the boy's straw-colored hair. Based on the tweenager's features and the appearance of the body Silvia Greene now unhappily inhabited, Jerzy surmised Brian got his dad's looks. "He's looking for your father. He's afraid he's, uh, violating the restraining order while masquerading as someone else. Has anyone strange contacted you?"

Brian shook his head. "Naw, no grownup I don't already know."

Dr. Teagle whirled on Jerzy. "There, see, nothing to worry about."

"And your younger son?" Jerzy pressed.

The woman's face, until then, a rigid mask of self-righteous indignation, suddenly crumpled. She burst into hysterical tears and, sobbing, staggered off into the dim interior of the house. Gob-smacked, Jerzy followed the woman with his gaze then turned to the boy. "W-what was that all about?"

Brian, his face flushed—with anger, grief, or just plain embarrassment—glared at Jerzy. "My brother's in the hospital," he ground out between clenched teeth.

"I'm sorry about that," Jerzy offered genuine sympathy. "I hope he gets well ..."

Brian cut him off. "Gabe ain't gettin' better. He's in what they call 'palliative care.'" The boy made air quotes then slammed the door in Jerzy's face.

* * *

The nurse at the ward's station, a bright-eyed woman of color whose nametag read "Ellen Mayhew," looked up from the photograph. "Yes, I recognize her. That's Consuelo Garcia—a new volunteer, just started working with patients."

"People actually *volunteer* to work with dying kids?" Jerzy shook his head. "God love 'em." He didn't clarify whether he meant the volunteers or the children.

"It's very satisfying work," Ellen observed, sizing Jerzy up. "You look like a nice, compassionate person," she added slyly, "just the sort who volunteers." She offered a dazzling, encouraging smile.

"I'll, uh, consider it, but, in the meantime, can you tell me when Consuelo's next scheduled to be here?"

The woman tutted as she consulted a tablet on the desk, "And how do you know Consuelo?" she asked, clearly trying to sound casual but just as clearly curious about Jerzy's interest.

"She and I worked for the same agency. In fact, we did the same job."

"Really?" Ellen sounded relieved, as if she bought the explanation. "Looks like you're in luck, Mr. Petoskey. She's in today, right now, in fact."

"Great!" Jerzy smiled back, though he doubted his smile dazzled as much as Ellen's. "Where can I find her?"

The woman shook her head. "I'm sorry, only relatives of patients or volunteers are allowed on the ward. However," she looked up and grinned at Jerzy. "I'd be happy to take a *prospective* volunteer for a tour."

"Lead on," Jerzy waved his hand down the hall.

* * *

Despite his years in espionage and, later, law enforcement, Jerzy winced at the sight of young kids, who ought to be running around outdoors, instead hunched over in wheelchairs like seniors, hooked up to IV's and monitors. Ellen, of course, didn't appear in the last phased, cheerfully greeting patients right and left. After a long walk down sterile-looking halls, they came to a brightly lit atrium where both patients and visitors sat at picnic tables surrounded by potted plants.

"I don't see Consuelo," Ellen grunted as she surveyed the occupants of the atrium. "But this is where the volunteers and patients meet."

"I've got a hunch," Jerzy offered. "Do you have a patient here named Gabe Teagle?"

Ellen consulted the tablet, which she'd tucked under her arm as they left the nurse's station. "Yes, we do. Why do you ask?"

"Because if we check his room, I bet we'll find Consuelo."

In fact, as they approached the room to which Ellen led Jerzy, a Latina stepped out of it, carefully closing the door behind her, so as not to disturb a sleeping occupant.

"Ms. Garcia?" Jerzy ventured at the woman's back.

She whirled, startled. "Do I know you?" she asked.

Jerzy offered her his hand. "We worked for the same boss."

She took it, and, when Jerzy traced the sign on her palm with his forefinger, her Adam's apple bobbed slightly with recognition. "Yes, we did," she hissed.

"Well, since you two know each other," Ellen chuckled good-naturedly, blissfully unaware of the sudden tension between Consuelo and Jerzy. "I'll leave you to it." She disappeared down the hall.

Kent glared at Jerzy. "Did the Agency send you?" he snapped.

"Not directly," Jerzy shrugged, attempting to be relaxed and mild-mannered, though his guts roiled, "but they helped me find you. DEV hired me. Mrs. Greene wants her body back *now*." He stared into Silvia's brown eyes, trying to reach Kent.

Kent spun on Silvia's heel and began walking down the hall, stylish but sensible black flats clicking on the linoleum. "Silvia can wait," he huffed over her shoulder.

Jerzy pursued the retreating body bandit with quiet determination. "Mrs. Greene is highly dysphoric," he insisted.

Kent snorted, neither turning nor slowing the pace. "*I'm* supposed to be concerned about *her* pain?"

"It's her body, after all." Jerzy fought to keep his voice level and calm. No point in making a scene. The fewer questions asked by security here at Children's National Hospital the better.

"She'll get it back soon enough," Kent sniffed dismissively. "I'm never getting my son back," he unsuccessfully choked down a sob.

Jerzy reached out and grabbed Kent by the sleeve of his smart, feminine blazer. He whirled; the face he wore—Silvia's—warred between outrage and grief, teeth gritted as tears tracked her cheeks. The sight stirred unbidden memories in Jerzy—like his instructors at the Agency warning about the abrupt switch from a body inured to testosterone to one drenched in estrogen and the challenges that presented to emotional control, a vital tool for any clandestine operative. Jerzy never found that an issue, though. He cried as easily under a full load of testosterone as he did with estrogen.

"Look, I get it," he said as gently as possible, keeping his voice low, if urgent. "Your ex has got the court in her pocket. They're eating up all her lies, and, by the time that judge sees sense and lets you see your kids as you, as Kent, as their father, it'll be too late—for Gabe, at least. In Silvia's body, you can fool them into thinking you're just some sweet old lady named Consuelo who wants to cheer up sick kids, and you can actually see your son before the end, even if not as you."

Kent bit Silvia's lip as the tears continued to leak from her eyes. "There's a 'but' there, in what you're saying. I hear it. What's the 'but?'"

Jerzy shook his head. "There's no 'but,' Kent. Look, as miserable as Mrs. Greene is, it won't kill her if she doesn't get her body back for a few more hours."

"A few more hours?" Kent sobbed. "He's sleeping! They're not sparing the morphine at this late stage, and it knocks him out. No telling when he'll wake again!"

Jerzy dropped Kent's sleeve and stood back. "When my kids were that age, I sat and watched them sleep for hours."

Kent swallowed hard. "How old are they now?"

"Both in their twenties and away." He fixed Kent with a direct gaze. "So I know how precious time is when they're only 10."

"Only 10," Kent sobbed with renewed violence. "Gabe'll never see 11."

Jerzy reached out and put his arm across the shaking slender shoulders of the woman's body. "Come on, let's go back to his room …" He steered Kent in that direction and started a stately walk down the hall.

By the time they got to the door of Gabe's room, Kent's sobs no longer wracked Silvia. "I'll go in alone," he sniffed as he dabbed at her eyes with her right hand and wrapped the immaculately manicured fingers of her left around the handle.

Jerzy shook his head firmly. "Not a good idea."

"Why not?" Kent husked, some of the earlier fight returning to Silvia's voice. "You think I'm going to run?"

"No," Jerzy replied firmly, patiently, "because no one in your situation should be alone at a time like this."

"What do you know about my situation?" Kent nearly spat.

"Look," Jerzy dropped his voice again, "you know as well as I that only a handful of us have ever inhabited another person's body, and an even smaller group has crossed gender to do that. We're a very small sorority."

Kent fixed Silvia's brown, bloodshot eyes on Jerzy's. "And you're a member?"

Jerzy nodded. "We transgender body swappers have to stick together. No one else has our backs."

Kent sighed and pushed open the door. Jerzy followed on her heels into the sleeping darkness beyond.

Angling
Jacob Hazzard

This time I am a waitress, young and naive, kind and bashful, but I have been many other profiles. I find it alluring what prey they choose to pursue. Sometimes it's widows. Or blondes between the ages of 24-38. Or Black home cleaners. It's almost always women, though I have been a young homosexual male. And it's always someone seen as "vulnerable" to my malevolent morsels.

This one is a white man in his 40s, which statistically speaking, makes sense because around ninety percent of them are men and roughly half are white. I have had one woman. It was exhilarating just for the change in texture alone.

He draws on a cigarette, the ember casting a faint light across his face as we drive down a dark rural highway. He is tall, and lanky. He wears a brown leather jacket over a stained yellow button up where the buttons are misaligned. His hair is long and unkempt and he looks like someone out of a 70s cop show. His jawline is stubbly and sharp and his cheeks are sunken in as though he's always inhaling on his cigarette. I pretend to cough at the smoke, though it doesn't bother me.

He glances over at me and gives me a yellowing smile and says, "Sorry, I didn't know it agitated you. I can put it out."

I smile with only my lips and blink up at him, my hands clasped innocently on my lap and I say, "Oh. If you don't mind."

His smile widens, I can tell it arouses him, this innocence act. Contrary to popular belief from documentaries, this ritual isn't usually about sex. Sometimes it's motivated by anger or thrill or attention seeking. But sometimes it is about sex, such as in this case. Regardless, there is always some element of power, either regaining or projecting power.

They think what they do gives them power, but it's a false sense. What is true power? *I* am the one with power. I watch and I wait and I toy with them. I let them bluster and dance, and I am the one that says when it ends.

"Sure, sugar, I can do that." He flicks the still burning butt out the cracked window and leers at me through his coke bottle glasses, knowing I owe him because he did me a favor. "You are really going to like my dog."

I smile with my teeth this time and my face brightens at the mention of the K-9. The dog is his promise, the thing that got me into his car. Most have a promise: money, drugs, or sometimes the opportunity to help by feigning distress. Whatever it is they use to lure their victims away from where they make contact. In this case, he had asked me if I liked dogs and I replied, "Of course."

I hope the others weren't this stupid, getting into the car with a man old enough to be their father just to meet his dog. I push the thought out of my mind, it risks me blowing my cover if I get angry too early.

We ride in his rusted '93 Malibu in silence, dark trees on either side of the road. The tick sound of small bugs hitting the grill or windshield periodically sounds like popcorn left too long in the microwave. The car vibrates slightly from the old motor and uneven roads. I notice him licking his lips and running his hand through his greasy bangs as they fall into his eyes: he's nervous. I can't risk him giving up on me now. To play my part more accurately, I should be more chatty.

"It's really nice of you to let me meet your dog. Ever since Buddy was hit on highway 67 last month, I have been missing those doggy cuddles." That got him to relax. They love feeling like they are doing something nice for you.

"How long have you worked at Luella's? I haven't seen you there before. And I would have noticed you." Another yellow smile.

I blush at the attention and play dumb. I say, "Um...I guess it's been about three weeks now. My dad made me get a job the moment I turned 16, even though he doesn't work." I let out a little sigh then say, "It's really hard sometimes, but Lu is real nice."

The person I work with on these jobs, Agent Briarson, helps me locate targets. This time teenage waitresses at greasy spoon diners have been going missing all over the state of Alabama. The two of us narrowed down the search to three counties and Luella's was damn near the center.

I do this work all over the US, and the agent and I have talked about moving internationally. There are anywhere between 25 and 50 active here in the US at any given time, though the numbers are likely going down. Briarson doesn't fully know what I am, and she doesn't ask; she just wants them to be stopped and doesn't want the red tape of the justice system slowing down our work. So, she sends me a profile, we make a plan, and then I bait the hook. A good angler knows patience, and I am ever so patient.

The turn signal clacks in rhythm, a heartbeat that nearly matches the pace of the man's own heart. I can hear it, just as I can smell the pungent pheromones wafting off of him. Things the other victims couldn't possibly detect. The man is thrilled and he reeks of sweat and anticipation, and it's exactly where I want him.

We are headed down a road twisting between the trees that is so far out it doesn't have painted lines. After a few more minutes he turns into a driveway to a one story ranch house offset from the road. The kind of place you wouldn't even notice if you were driving by. The windows are dark: no lights are on. A rotting two rail wooden fence runs the length of the yard desperately in need of a cut. Many of the rails are broken and resting in the dirt like some teeth of a great beast.

We exit the car and the gravel crunches under our feet. He says, "It ain't much but it's home." I don't know if he expects me to respond but I don't say anything. He leads us to the front door which is a white screen door that creaks as he pulls it open. He clicks on the lights which are almost blinding coming in from the dark.

My eyes adjust and I look around the space. Old magazines, half empty bottles turned ash trays, and dirty dishes are piled around the room on any unoccupied space. The place smells of nicotine and musk. He makes an attempt to shuffle things around mumbling something about not expecting company though whatever he is doing isn't making anything appear cleaner. I decide to keep my shoes on.

He tries to be subtle and slides behind me. I hear the snick of the lock on the door. He smooths back his hair and says, "Can't be too careful these days." I nod in acknowledgement, and he wears the relief of me buying his flimsy excuse on his face.

"Would you like a drink?" he says too casually.

"Sure. But not too much because I don't drink often. And my dad will smell it on my breath," I say.

We move into the kitchen and I wonder if his cabinets are empty because of more stacks of dirty dishes on most surfaces. He pulls some cheap screwtop wine out of the vintage rounded refrigerator. Glancing around the room I ask, "So where is your dog?"

He pauses his pouring slightly before answering. "She has to be kept downstairs so she doesn't bark all the time. Wine?"

He hands me a drinking glass full of wine and I take it gingerly, sipping at the cool liquid. I ask, "Is there anyone else here?"

He shakes his head and says, "Just me and Daisy."

Good, that makes things easier. Despite popular opinion, many of them aren't loners. Sometimes they have families and "normal" lives they keep separate from their dark secrets. One such instance, a teenage child walked in as I was finishing. I stared unsure what might happen next, but the child just nodded at me as though they accepted what was happening as inevitable and slowly closed the door, not making a sound.

"How are you enjoying the wine?" He asks after too much silence.

I giggle and say, "It tickles my nose!" He has put some sort of tranquilizer in my drink, perhaps even Gamma-hydroxybutyrate, but I can taste the saltiness. Fortunately for me, my metabolism processes it so quickly, I hardly notice the effects.

He tries to make small talk but mostly he just points to things and tells me about them like a child with a bug collection. I fake a yawn and say, "It's getting late. Maybe I should go home."

He takes the glass from my hands and says, "Oh not until you've met Daisy. Let's go to the basement." He leads me to another door, one that is locked in three places. He removes the lock and gestures for me to start moving down the steps. "Daisy girl, you be good, we are coming down."

Pretending to be overwhelmed by whatever he slipped me, I move to take a step but falter, and instead sit down on the top step. "I don't feel well, Dale. I think I probably ought to go." I make to get up but a firm hand on my shoulder pushes me back down.

"No, I don't think so. I really need you to see what is in the basement. Let me help you."

He puts his hands under my armpits and lifts me up, carrying me down the steps, my feet barely scraping each step.

The darkness in the basement is oppressive and the smell is suffocating. The scent is sterile and smells of ammonia, something more akin to a hospital than a basement. It burns my nose as I inhale and I'm barely able to keep myself from retching. He reaches up and pulls a chain casting the room in the brightness of a swinging light.

The basement is half finished and the floor is sloped cement with a drain in the center. The room is sparsely furnished and has wood paneling on three sides. The light casts off a wall of sharp, silver reflections. Blunt instruments. So, it is more than just sex with this one.

Somehow my hands have found themselves behind my back while I am surveying the room. Something bites into my wrists and I hear the tent door sound of a zip tie.

"Dale, what are you doing?" I try to make myself sound scared and unsure, as though I don't know what's happening yet.

"Shut the fuck up. And don't scream." I can tell he wants me to scream, so I do. High pitched and hysterical, I could win an oscar. He hits me across the face with the flat of his hand and I can see his front lip lifting in the middle, quivering and barely showing his teeth. He is practically drooling with anticipation of how this will go, this fucking animal.

It's exactly how I want him. I want him to think he is in control, that this is just another routine, another urge satisfied. This is what makes them taste the best.

He throws me onto a retro moth-eaten couch and heads towards the wall of silver. I look over and there is a poorly taxidermied rottweiler sitting nearby, forever posed with her head cocked sideways as thoughts she's waiting for a treat. Daisy, poor girl.

The couch is repugnant, I can smell the offal and piss of his previous victims having soaked into its cushions; it only steadies my resolve. Looking at the ceiling I see what could be a contemporary art piece. I wait for the light to complete its arc and it illuminates the planks of the floor above. There are petite fingers nailed there, hodgepodge, pointing in different directions. If there is a pattern, I can't discern it. There are 14 in all.

Briarson has been good to me. My kind has always preyed upon humans since they were living in caves. Eventually, killings created too much unwanted attention and many of my kind were driven off and killed. We learned to source prey elsewhere and lived amongst the humans. Every once in a while, one of us slips up and gives into the craving, the deep well that drives our hunger, but they must be put down so the rest of us might survive. I found a way around it, a way to sate my desire and keep away the humans with torches.

My fingers extend and grow and my wrists swell. The plastic holding my arms snap as they grow and change. My feet go through a similar expansion and my jaw twists and widens allowing for the rows of teeth to fully form. The clothing tears away and my skin roils and darkens, the muscles filling out underneath.

He has finally chosen his instrument, a long metal rod with a solid metal sphere the size of a baseball on the end. Three sharp points stick out at odd angles. He turns and sees my seven foot height standing between him and the stairway leading out. He swallows hard.

The reveal is my favorite part besides the actual eating. Some beg, some fight, some faint, the last being my least favorite. I like to toy with them, often in the same way as their victims. I don't know how to explain it, but poetic justice tastes sweeter.

I take a step forward and he screams. To his credit, he swings the instrument at me and I catch it in my claws and snap it in half. He pisses himself, but I don't mind, it's all part of the ritual.

* * *

When I'm finished and wiping my mouth, I hear a pathetic whimper from behind a closed door. Another victim? It's not like them to bring another home while not finished with the last. I gently push the door open while I debate another course or a miracle for the victim. I am greeted by a whimper and two wet brown eyes. An emaciated pooch is chained to the wall, its ribs looking like spindles on an old wooden chair stretched under its patchy fur.

An hour later I am hitchhiking as someone else, Daisy II held under my arm. I make myself another young woman, someone more likely to be offered a ride. I found a set of clothing in a garbage bag in the basement from one of the other victims in my new companion's room. I am full, but never satisfied. I am already thinking about the next target. Briarson mentioned that there have been overnight nurses in the Detroit area going missing at too high of a rate to be coincidence. I begin developing my next character and make my way north.

Who?

After a long and successful career as a software developer and technical architect, **David Castlewitz** turned to a first love: writing fiction, particularly SF, fantasy, magical realism, and light horror. His stories have appeared in many anthologies and online as well as print publications. David lives on the North Shore, outside Chicago, where he enjoys long walks, the occasional bike ride, and other outdoor adventures. Story ideas come from all directions, often rooted in people – how they react and what they do. Tech is a backdrop.

Toni Artuso says: I am an emerging/aging trans female writer from Salem, MA. Recently retired from 30 years in educational publishing, I'm transitioning, as well as trying to accelerate the emerging and slow down the aging.

Rosie Oliver has been in love with science fiction ever since as a teenager she discovered a whole bookcase of yellow-covered Gollancz science fiction books in Chesterfield library in central England. It sent her on a world-spinning imaginary writing journey from the depths of Earth's oceans to multi-verses with varying time speeds. With her scientific background she tends to naturally focus on realistic future tech stories. 2023 saw her become a finalist in the Writers of the Future contest and her debut novel, 'Edge of Existence – C.A.T. novel', published.

Jacob Hazzard says: I am a software product manager and former academic that is working to turn his creative writing habit into something more full time.